STACEY KADE

BITTER PILL

A RENNIE HARLOW MYSTERY

STACEY KADE BOOKS

Original Copyright © 2007 by Stacey Klemstein

First Echelon Press paperback printing / 2007

Revised Edition Copyright © 2013 by Stacey Klemstein

Cover Design © Stacey Kade and Suzie Townsend

ISBN 9780988585942

PRINTED IN THE UNITED STATES OF AMERICA
10 9 8 7 6 5 4 3 2 1

PRAISE FOR STACEY KADE

"Stacey Kade crafts an action-packed and wildly romantic story about our desire to not only be seen but also understood. *The Rules* is a great read." —Rachel Cohn, best-selling author of *Beta* and *Gingerbread*

"I was immediately swept up in Ariane's story. Equal parts thrill-ride and love story, *The Rules* is intense and emotional. This book stays with you long after you finish." —Sophie Jordan, *New York Times* best-selling author of the Firelight series

"Readers will be unable to put down Kade's first Project Paper Doll title." —*RT Magazine* (April Top Pick, 4.5 Stars)

"*The Rules* covers a bit of everything from bullying, parental issues, romance, and more. Stacey Kade took real life issues and mixed it with a sci/fi feeling, and she pulled it off perfectly." —Good Choice Reading

"A wonderfully engaging story that left me with a book hangover." —Blue Sky Bookshelf on *The Rules*

"FINALLY! A science fiction book that does everything right for a change and it couldn't have come at a better time too." —Tales of the Inner Book Fanatic on *The Rules*

"One part romance, two parts sparring match, and it's toe-curlingly fantastic."—Refracted Light Reviews on *Body & Soul*

"It feels as though it's been a long time since I've had this much FUN reading a book!"—Paranormal Indulgence on *The Ghost and The Goth*

"So very rarely do I find a book that is so fun and humorous and energetic, but still has the surprising emotional depth to make me cry."—Stories & Sweeties on *Queen of the Dead*

Books by

STACEY KADE

THE GHOST AND THE GOTH SERIES

The Ghost and the Goth

Queen of the Dead

Body & Soul

PROJECT PAPER DOLL SERIES

The Rules

The Hunt

BITTER PILL

ONE

Don't misunderstand, it's not like I enjoyed having this happen to me. I guess it's just some kind of bizarre twist of fate, or maybe a sixth sense that only kicks in when the grim reaper is afoot. It's not like I'd wanted to find the high school swim coach floating face down in the deep end, any more than I'd wanted to find the assistant librarian hanging from the rafters in the library attic with a stack of true crime books kicked over beneath her.

It's just that whenever bodies started floating, swinging or, in this case, dropping, I happened to be there. Bad luck, maybe. Still, worse luck for them than for me. This time, it was some very poor fortune for Doc Hallacy, the pharmacist.

Doc's shop, a squat brick building with a striking orange and blue RX sign above the front door, sat on the corner of Main and First. On a Friday morning, at five minutes to eight, the main thoroughfare of Morrisville was deserted. Most of the stores didn't open until nine. So unless you needed Doc Hallacy, who opened promptly at eight as he had for more than forty years, you had no business on Main at that time of day.

I parked my silver BMW in one of the diagonal spots in front of the pharmacy. The sporty little coupe was one of the toys my ex-husband had purchased before deciding he was too young to settle down, four years into our marriage. I'd fought for and won the car in my settlement and took great pride in abusing it in his stead.

As I climbed out and slammed the door shut, Starbucks Breakfast Blend slopped over the edge of my travel mug and splattered on the side window, burning my fingers in the process. The pain was worth it. I grinned, imagining Jeff's expression of horror, as I watched the coffee trickle down the car door, creating clean streaks. I hadn't washed the car in more than a year, not since I'd moved home to Morrisville from Chicago. Nothing like being a scorned and divorced woman before the age of thirty to make you a little bitter.

With a deep sigh of satisfaction, I stepped over the curb and headed to Doc Hallacy's door to wait for him to flip the sign to OPEN and welcome me in.

I'll admit to being lost in my first cup of coffee of the day—Starbucks was a luxury that I hadn't quite been able to give up in my relocation—so I didn't notice anything out of the ordinary at first. As I stood there, enjoying the early May sunshine on my face and perusing the store window—hell of a deal on a walker/bath seat (Doc also sold medical supplies)—it gradually occurred to me that something wasn't right.

I pushed back my sleeve and checked my watch. Three minutes after eight. Suddenly that little voice in the back of my head, the one my mother encouraged me to ignore, piped up, offering all kinds of theories.

He could just be a little late, but in all these months of early morning pharmacy trips, he'd never been before. Maybe he was sick or hurt. Doc Hallacy was no fresh-faced pharmacology student anymore. He had to be pushing eighty, at least.

With the image of Doc unconscious and bleeding stuck in my head, I stepped up to the door and peered in through the glass panel. The door slipped open under the pressure of my hand cupped against the glass to block the light. I stepped back in shock. By now my little voice was screaming.

Clutching my travel mug, I crossed the threshold cautiously, noticing the lights were still off. "Now would be the time to call the Sheriff's Office," my mom would say. "Let them earn their money." But my relationship with the Sheriff's Office, particularly the Sheriff himself, was a little complicated at the moment. I had to make sure calling would be the right thing to do, not just what I wanted to do.

The familiar and comforting smell of the pharmacy—old building, dust, and talcum powder—filled my nose as I walked in farther. I passed the cash register and the metal rack of paperback books on my way to the counter in the back. I gave the dusty book covers a fond smile as I rounded the corner. This had been the only bookstore in town when I was a kid. Doc Hallacy's wife, Maybelle, had always tried to get something new in for me every week or so.

The store grew darker the deeper I headed in, and the familiar smell of the pharmacy started to mix with a new scent, one I'd recently come to know well. Fresh blood and the stench of death.

Hoping I was wrong, I stepped up to the darkened counter. The metal security gate was up, retracted into the ceiling. A faint bit of light shone through the frosted glass window set high on the back wall.

"Doc? You here?"

No answer. The smell had grown stronger, coating my nose and mouth. I swallowed hard and leaned over the counter to look into the back. The freestanding shelves of carefully labeled medicines seemed undisturbed, but the side door, which opened into a tiny hallway, leading to the storeroom and a delivery door in back, stood open.

I set my mug down on a nearby shelf of vitamins and leaned farther over the long counter, letting my feet come off the floor.

"Doc?" I called again. I tried to inch forward, but my palm

slipped on the slick counter. My feet flew up, tipping me farther forward. Only a quick grab kept me from falling into a heap on the other side. As it was, I ended up clinging to the counter's edge with my head upside down, which brought me face to face with a very dead Doc Hallacy.

He was lying on the floor, tucked underneath the countertop. Red marks smeared the floor where he'd been dragged. A metal cane, bloodied and bent, rested by his side. He'd been beaten to death. Blood pooled beneath his head...and his glasses, the little square spectacles he always wore on the tip of his nose, dangled from his face, the lenses shattered and the rims twisted. His eyes, already starting to cloud over, stared up at me.

I scrambled backward, knocking down cardboard drug displays. Once safely back on the customer side of the counter, I lifted a shaking hand to my mouth and swallowed the urge to throw up. Who could have done that to Doc? He'd run this place for more than forty years and he'd always had a kind word for everyone.

Tears swelled in my eyes. I couldn't think of anyone who'd...

A soft rustling sound emerged from somewhere in the store. Cold washed over me. Someone else was here. Maybe the someone who'd killed Doc.

I bolted for the door, forgoing any plans to appear cool and calm in the face of panic. Just before I pushed open the door to run out into the warm sunshine, a second noise reached my ears—the distinctive squeak and then slam of the delivery door in the back of the pharmacy. I'd certainly sat in here waiting for prescriptions often enough to recognize it.

I hurried to my car, my hand trembling as I tried to dig car keys from my pocket. I got the door unlocked and slid in, hitting the lock button before the door even closed.

I pulled my cell phone from the center console and punched in the number for the Sheriff's Office. Sad that I knew it so well.

"Morrisville Sheriff's Office," Sheryl Dupres, a deputy taking her shift as dispatcher and receptionist, answered. The official dispatcher/receptionist, the second one this year, had quit last month to move to Springfield. It was too boring here, she'd said. If only she'd waited a little while longer.

"Hey, Sheryl, it's me, Rennie." Sheryl had been my babysitter years ago. Once all these tight connections in a small town would have driven me crazy; now it offered a tiny measure of comfort.

"Hey, Rennie. Who's dead now?" she asked, laughing.

I sighed.

Sheryl went quiet. "You're kidding."

"No." I rubbed my forehead with my free hand. "It's Doc Hallacy."

Stunned silence followed, then a muffled curse. "I'll put you right through," she said, all joking gone from her tone.

I waited for Jake Bristol's deep, resonating voice with more anticipation than was right, even though he was bound to lecture me again about looking for trouble. Like I went searching for dead bodies. Like he had room to criticize.

I'd gone to high school with Bristol. Believe me, back in those days, he'd landed in more than his share of hot water. He'd been a senior when I was a freshman, and he'd been the one all the mothers warned about, while still feeling a little flutter inside themselves and longing to be sixteen again. He drove a motorcycle he'd restored, showed up late for class or not at all, and had an aura of defiance that, more often than not, got him sent to the principal's office when he hadn't even said a word. Immediately after high school graduation, he joined the Army. It changed him, gave him direction, I suppose. As he once explained to me, it wasn't that he'd hated authority before; just that he'd been given no reason to respect it. The Army had taken care of that real fast. He'd come back to Morrisville after completing his tour of duty, settling into small-town life again without a hitch.

Small-town married life, I reminded myself, feeling that painful tug in the general vicinity of my heart. We'd been nothing to each other before he left town, and we were nothing now...sort of. He was married to Margene Reynolds, a former homecoming queen, no less. However, that didn't mean I couldn't take some comfort or pleasure from hearing his voice, did it?

Sheryl got to him first.

"Dammit, Rennie," he greeted me.

"It's not my fault," I said instantly. "I just came to pick up my mom's prescription and I noticed the door was unlocked, but the lights were still off."

"You should have called right then," he said. I imagined him sitting in the cracked and worn leather chair behind his desk, running his hand over his close-cropped dark hair in frustration, something he did frequently around me.

"I didn't know anything was wrong," I protested.

"It's you, Rennie. Of course, something's wrong."

I tried not to feel hurt by that. "Anyway, I found him behind the counter, kind of hidden back there."

Bristol sighed.

"I think somebody beat him to death." I thought back on the scene for a second. "One of those metal canes he sells was back there, too."

"All right, I'll send someone over—"

"But Bristol, I heard the back door open and shut. I think whoever did it is still around here somewhere." I looked out my car windows, but I was still the only one on the street. I wasn't sure if that was comforting or not.

His tone sharpened. "I'm coming now." I heard the distinctive clunking of him putting on his gun belt. "Stay out of the store and—"

"Don't touch anything," I finished for him. "I know. It's not like I've never found a body before, Bristol."

"Believe me, I know." He didn't sound happy. Then he hung up.

I kept my phone in hand, double-checked my door locks, and waited for help to arrive. I didn't have to wait long.

TWO

I notice things other people don't. That's really all it boils down to. That, and I'm cursed with an overactive and overly accurate imagination. No one, especially the police, ever wants to believe that, even though it's the truth. When I lived in my first apartment in Chicago, I was the only one who noticed the mail spilling out of the mailbox for 3E and thought anything of it. Everyone else assumed the horrible smell emanating from the third floor was another poor squirrel that had found its way into the heating vents and couldn't find the way back out, just like the summer before. They weren't far from wrong. It did smell about the same, only it lasted a lot longer, much the way you'd expect if the squirrel was 5'11 and 190 lbs.

In high school, I could always tell who'd hooked up the weekend before; their body language screamed it even if they said nothing at all to each other. That meant I was also usually the first to know who was pregnant.

In grade school, I busted John Walsh as the culprit stealing from the Sunday School offering when he gave Shannon Moyer five dollars all in quarters to lift up her skirt.

I see something that seems strange or off in some way and then the connections start firing, coming up with all kinds of possibilities. Most of the time, it's stupid stuff, and it doesn't matter if I'm right or wrong. I mean, who cares if young Widow Pearson is having an affair with the bag boy at the IGA? It's so very clearly mutual, and judging by the sad attempt at a mustache and the pack of cigarettes in his shirt pocket, the kid is old enough to consent.

Then there are the other times, like when I found Coach Swenson dead in the pool on my first day of substitute teaching at Morrisville High, or when Esther Harris, Chief Librarian, directed me to the attic storage area of the library for some research materials and I found the assistant librarian, Janice Parsmouth, hanging from a rope she'd flung over a rafter, her granny panties down around her knees. Those are the times when my being right or wrong matters a whole bunch because finding out what really happened is usually the only way to get my name off the suspect list.

My discovery of Doc Hallacy's death—no, murder—was more than enough to put me at the top of yet another of those lists. My only consolation was that I now had a legitimate reason for wanting to talk to the sheriff at every opportunity.

About three minutes after I hung up with Bristol, a squad car pulled up next to the curb about a half block away from me and the pharmacy, obviously trying not to scare away the murderer, if he/she had stuck around.

A sudden tap on my side window nearly sent me through the sun roof. I turned to see Bristol's face inches from mine, his mouth tight and turned down. He was one of those rare men who improved with age. He still had a full head of dark hair, now mixed with a little silver at the temples. His lean form from high school had filled in at the shoulders but not at the belly. I loved the little lines at the corners of his eyes, just slivers of white skin in his tanned face. He got that tan from spending every spare moment pushing wood at his father's lumberyard.

He pointed to me and then held his hand up, palm facing me. *Stay here.*

Heart still palpitating, I nodded.

He approached the pharmacy, pressing his back against the wall of the neighboring shoe store, Sole Mate. He shoved open the pharmacy's door with one hand, his gun out in the other, and disappeared into the darkness of the store.

I waited with my nerves on edge, prepared to jump at the sound of gunshots. After a few minutes, the lights in the pharmacy snapped on, and Bristol came back out the door. He paused when he saw me watching him and shook his head, his mouth pulled even tighter than before. Empty, I guess. No convenient murder suspect hanging around, other than me, of course.

In my rearview mirror, I watched Bristol head to a squad car parked on the opposite side of the street behind me. No wonder I hadn't seen him arrive—he'd sent the deputy one way and he'd come around the other, an attempt to keep the murderer from escaping, probably. Obviously, they'd been a little too late for that plan. He opened the driver's side door and let it hang open as he reached in for something.

Radioing dispatch to let them know not to hurry with the ambulance, probably. I grimaced. Flipping open the storage area under the armrest, I pulled out the jumbo-sized bottle of hand sanitizer my mother had insisted I carry with me at all times. For once, I was grateful. Even though I hadn't really touched anything, just thinking about what happened in the pharmacy set off a powerful urge to clean my hands. God, I hoped that didn't mean I was turning into her.

Just after I poured a huge blob of the solution into my palm, my cell phone rang, startling me. I'd tucked it under my leg to keep it in close reach, a habit from my Chicago commuting days. After extricating the phone, I clicked "Answer Call" gingerly and braced the phone between my ear and shoulder. "Hello?"

"Please, please tell me that is you, my favorite freelance

reporter, in the center of that police frenzy down there," Max Biddleman, editor of the Morrisville *Gazette* and my sometimes boss, greeted me. The *Gazette* office was just up the street, diagonal from the courthouse and Civil War memorial in the town square. Max could probably see everything from the front window.

I rubbed the cold, slippery sanitizer over my hands and watched Trent Sheffey, one of Bristol's deputies, block off the entrance to the pharmacy with bright yellow crime scene tape. Only in Morrisville would this be considered a police frenzy. "Not now, Max," I said. "Doc Hallacy's dead, murdered, it looks like."

"Oh, God," Max said. He managed about three seconds of respectful silence before he continued. "Please tell me you're the one who found him."

Max loved me for the same reason Bristol had developed an intense, professional dislike for me—I always seemed to find myself in the thick of things. Max loved me because I sold papers. Rather, the trouble I always managed to find myself in sold papers.

"You're a ghoul, you know that? A man is dead."

"You did, didn't you?"

I sighed. "Yeah." Hands now clean and dry, I yanked at a loose thread in the leather steering wrap, winding it around my fingers as it unraveled.

"Yes!" He practically shouted with delight. I pictured him in my mind, a balding, middle-aged, gay man, his feet propped up on paper-covered desk. The gay part, I guess, was more speculation on my part than anything, but he always said 'we' when he talked about his weekends, and no one had ever seen him with anyone. Plus, why else does a liberal man move from San Francisco to a small town in southern Illinois but for love?

"All right, here's the deal," he said sharply, his tone changing from joy to business in a heartbeat. "I'll pay you to write the story

11

about finding him—those always play well. But I'll cover the tribute article myself."

Tribute articles were a big deal in Morrisville and a unique ritual as far as I knew. When someone died here, more often than not, they already had something written, rough form, for their own tribute, an extended obituary essentially. Six inches above the fold on the front page, right next to the headline, listing every major accomplishment in said life and glossing over the flaws in a highly complimentary manner. Heaven help us when two people died in Morrisville on the same day. It was a battle to win the place of the tribute article. Ultimately, Max made the decision, despite a surprising amount of lobbying done by some family members. Sometimes the celebrity of one corpse would win out over another. Other times, like today, the sheer violence of the death would win the day.

I steeled myself for another round of negotiations with Max. "I want both. The tribute article and the discovery story."

"Rennie–"

"I'm the one who found him, and you know if I write both, it'll sell better." I hated doing this, turning someone's death into a commodity, but Max left me with no choice. To beat him at this game, I had to think like he did. I had to out-Max Max.

When I'd first come to town a year ago, he'd refused to hire me as a reporter for the *Gazette*. I couldn't exactly blame him. My last journalism experience had been a course in my freshman year at UW-Madison. But when I'd become one of the prime suspects in Coach Swenson's murder and offered to write about it for the *Gazette*, Max had suddenly become very open to the idea of a freelance reporter. I'd been cleared of any wrong-doing, obviously, and my story had contributed to the best sales in *Gazette* history, but Max still wouldn't hire me full-time. Now it was just because he was cheap, rather than there being any doubt of my talent.

I'd found a few other clients who needed my writing and marketing background, and I managed to scrape by every month. Max gave me pretty regular, if boring, assignments, which helped my money situation, but I needed more if I was ever going to make a real life here. Yeah, I'd wrung a healthy alimony from Jeff, taking advantage of his eagerness to be free of me and my demanding monogamy, but I was saving it all. One day I'd have a glorious bonfire with it in front of him. Or maybe I'd donate it to a charity he hated and direct them to send the receipt to him. Either way, I couldn't bring myself to spend it. Not yet. It was tainted. Spending it would mean what he'd done was okay, that you could treat someone like he'd treated me and throw money at it to make it all go away.

"I'm not hiring you full time," Max said.

"I didn't ask you to." Though, that was always the subtext of this conversation. "I'm just talking about these two stories." I waited for a second and then wearily added the words that I knew would push him over the edge. "Unless you want me to write them for Litchfield." *The Litchfield Courier* was Max's nearest, and pretty much only, competition.

"Just get in here as soon as you can," he said sharply. He sounded grumpy, but I knew him well enough by now to know that for some reason, he actually enjoyed this repetitive back and forth between us.

"Won't be till this afternoon now." I watched Bristol close up his car and head back this way. "I'll have to make a statement, and then you know I have to interview Mrs. Mayor yet this morning."

"Ah, yes, the 75th Annual Ladies of Morrisville Garden Club Show. Scintillating business," he said.

"You assigned me to it," I reminded him.

"Well, what there is of it, cover well." He paused, then said, "See what dirt you can dig up on Hallacy while you're there."

I grimaced. "Not everyone has skeletons, Max."

"Yes, they do, and you know it. Did it look like a robbery in there?"

I thought about it. "No," I admitted. "Everything looked pretty much in place and the cash register wasn't messed with."

"Skeletons. I'm telling you."

I started to argue. "Just because that would make for a better story—"

Bristol knocked on my window again.

"I've got to go, Max." I ended the call and pushed the button to lower the window.

Bristol handed in a thermos lid of coffee to me.

"Thanks." I wrapped my hands around it gratefully. I'd lost my beloved travel mug of Starbucks in the store somewhere. Knowing the Sheriff's Office, this wasn't Starbucks, but in an emergency, it was close enough.

"You all right?" He bent over and rested his arm on my door.

"Yeah, I guess. Just shook up a bit." I took a sip of coffee, watching him out of the corner of my eye.

Despite the circumstances, a warm little flutter spread through my chest, just being this close to him. He and I'd spent way too much time together in the last six months. Granted, he'd been the law and I the suspected criminal, but he'd been honest and fair, not to mention more than a touch compassionate, during that whole terrible episode. I'd lusted after him in high school, intrigued by the hint of danger that always seemed to surround him, just like every other girl above the age of thirteen. Now, I yearned to be around him, to see him smile, or tell me about his day. He'd done some of that even when I hadn't quite been cleared yet. Crazy as it sounds, when I was cleared, I'd been more than a little sorry. It meant my daily conversations and interactions with one Jake Bristol, the best man I knew, were over.

"You want to tell me what happened?" he asked.

"It's like I told you. When Doc didn't open the pharmacy in time, I went in to make sure he was okay." I shifted in my seat uncomfortably. "I thought maybe he'd fallen and hit his head or broken his hip or something. He's not exactly a young guy, you know? I mean…he *wasn't* a young guy."

Bristol rubbed his face wearily, then stared at me, his warm brown eyes too intense. "How do you get yourself into this? The first person found on the scene is usually a viable suspect for the murder. But not in this town, not with you."

"I can't help it, it just happens." I tried not to sound too plaintive.

"No, Rennie, lightning strikes just happen." He shook his head with a tight smile. "You are a walking disaster."

Stung, I shoved the thermos lid back at him, sloshing coffee onto the leather interior, and jabbed my car keys into the ignition. "Screw you, Bristol."

He sighed. "Rennie…"

"What?" I jerked the gearshift into reverse.

He started to say something then shook his head. "I'm going to need you to come in to make an official statement."

"Not till this afternoon." I lifted my chin defiantly, daring him to challenge me. "I have to get home to explain to my mother that she'll have to wait for her prescription and then I've got an interview with Gloria Lottich."

"Fine. We've already got your prints on file, so we can rule out anything you touched." His mouth tightened and he hesitated for the slightest of seconds. "We're going to need your shirt."

"What? Why?" I looked down at myself and saw, for the first time, a splotch of blood shaped like a tear drop on the stomach of my pale blue t-shirt.

"Crime lab will want to make sure that's Doc's blood and not the killer's."

I swallowed hard, struggling against the urge to pluck the fabric away from my skin. "So, I'm just supposed to drive home topless? This is Morrisville. There are laws about how long Christmas decorations can stay up. You're telling me there are no ordinances about half-naked driving?" I asked, discomfort setting my tone a little too close to rude.

He walked back to his squad car, tossing out the remains of the coffee in the thermos lid on the way. He returned with a paper bag and a bright blue bundle of fabric. The fabric, a t-shirt, he handed to me, while he held onto the bag.

I put the car back into park and unfolded the t-shirt. The front had a small patch of writing over the left side in the shape of star. Morrisville Sheriff's Office, it read. Interdepartmental Softball League. I flipped it over to look at the back. Bristol 17.

"Your softball shirt?" I asked. God help me, despite the circumstances, I loved the idea of his name on my back, his shirt against my skin. *Bad, Rennie. Bad, bad.*

He shrugged. "Unless you have a better idea."

I shook my head. He stood and turned his back toward the window, blocking the view from the side of the car. That helped, but it didn't keep anyone from looking through the windshield. I sighed. Oh, well, what little I had, they were welcome to see. Besides, Deputy Sheffey appeared to be occupied with taking notes anyway, and the first curiosity-seekers on the scene had their attention focused on the pharmacy door, now blocked off with crime tape.

I yanked the bloodied shirt off over my head, silently thanking whatever voice of caution in my brain had urged me to wear proper undergarments this morning. Much to my chagrin, bras were more wishful thinking on my part than a strict necessity. However, it would have been nice if the voice of caution had also recommended a little more time on my hair this morning—I could feel it standing up in messy spikes, like a blonde tumbleweed on top of my head. Very attractive.

I thrust my arms through Bristol's t-shirt. The familiar smell of him, the clean scent of his clothing, surrounded me. I tugged the rest of the shirt down into place, loving the feel of it against my skin even as I knew it was wrong. After all, Bristol's shirt smelled good, like him, because it had been recently laundered…by his wife, Margene.

Without thinking, I bumped his arm with the back of my hand to let him know I'd completed my wardrobe change. As usual, he'd rolled his shirt sleeves up, revealing tanned and strong forearms. I jolted slightly at the warmth of his skin against mine, and my heart flipped up and twisted in my chest, like a paper cutout on a string in the breeze

Bristol turned around and opened the paper bag. I dropped my bloodied shirt inside.

"So, how's Margene?" I asked Bristol, as I always did when I started having trouble remembering he was married.

His face closed down, like he'd shut some internal door against me. "Fine." He didn't really sound surprised at the strange conversation twist I'd thrown him. "Getting ready for the Garden Show." He closed up the top of the bag with precise, crisp folds in the paper.

"Right," I said. Margene had been more than happy to settle into her role of Mrs. Sheriff, second only to Mrs. Mayor, Gloria

Lottich. Margene and I'd also gone to school together, although she was a couple years younger than me. She'd moved to town in the seventh grade when her father took a job at the propane factory. By her junior year in high school, she'd worked her way up from trailer trash to co-captain of the varsity cheerleading team, second only to Laura Brown. Apparently, Margene's ambition had limits. Word was, she'd caught wind of Jake's upwardly mobile plans as soon as he'd returned to town from the Army and she'd trapped him with her reportedly magnificent thighs. Chelsea was born barely inside of wedlock, and then all Margene had to do was sit back and wait while Jake's star kept rising.

"And Chelsea?" I asked.

"Finishing fifth grade in a couple weeks." He frowned at me, highlighting those marvelous wrinkles near his eyes.

Time to change the subject again. "What about Max?" I asked.

"Max," he repeated with a frown.

"Yeah. Editor of the *Gazette*, nosiest human being alive?" I waited for some flicker of recognition from Bristol and got a grim nod. "He's going to want details for a story. Time of death, potential motives, the weapon…"

Bristol frowned. "I don't want to share any of that information with the public just yet. Incidentally, I think you're right about the cane being the murder weapon." His eyes dropped to the phone in my lap. "I don't want that part in the paper, got it?" He rubbed his face, the stubble on his chin making a rasping sound against his hand. "I'd rather not have anything in the paper just yet."

I shook my head. "Max is sitting right over there." I pointed at the *Gazette* office. "It's not like he can't see it for himself. You know him, he'll print something. Better he get most of the facts from a reliable source."

"You run all of it past me before anything hits the printer," he said.

I made an exasperated sound. "We've been through this before. I get the lecture from you about responsible media. Then I turn around and get the freedom of the press speech from Max." I glowered at him. "I should put the two of you in a room together and let you duke it out."

Bristol's mouth twitched upward in a smile. "Wouldn't be fair."

"Why not?"

"Max could convince a snake to go vegetarian. I just have a gun."

I pretended to consider his words. "True enough. I guess my money's still safe on Max."

"Oh, ha, ha."

I smiled at him reluctantly. "I'll see you this afternoon." I shifted the car into reverse and waited for him to step back.

"Wait. One more thing." He reached into his pocket and handed something to me. A little orange-brown bottle of pills. The label read, 'Irene Harlow, 643 Fairlane Rd, Take one a day for Narcolepsy, as needed. Dr. E. Murphy.' I snapped the top off to find her normal anti-anxiety drugs inside. Thank goodness for Doc Hallacy conspiring with Dr. Murphy. She'd have been to a half a dozen physicians by now, if neither of them had listened to her as attentively as they did. Now, with Doc Hallacy gone, I didn't know how I was going to handle my mom. A twinge of self-pity snapped me back to the reality of the situation. Doc Hallacy was dead. My problems were nothing compared to that.

"Thank you." I clutched the bottle. "That was…kind of you." And a bit unethical. Anything in the pharmacy was probably technically part of a crime scene.

"He'd already filled it and set it out for you on the back

counter," Bristol said. "I'll make note of it in my report that I released it for urgent medical need. You should have the contents checked with the pharmacist at the hospital just to be sure."

"It's the right stuff. I recognize the numbers on the pill." I started to touch his arm but stopped myself just in time. "Thank you again."

He nodded. "She's better now that you're here." With that he pulled up and walked away.

I watched him go, my chest tight with guilt and some kind of desperate hope. Why did everything have to be so complicated?

With no quick answers in sight, I pulled out and went home.

THREE

"Mom?" "Mom?" I called into the house as I walked in the back door. "I'm back."

I checked the rear bedroom—my childhood room, now her sewing room—only to find it dark and empty, the Singer still covered in its protective plastic. The kitchen, where I stopped to wash my hands, was deserted, just like the small dining area and family room beyond it.

Letting air out through my teeth, I headed to her bedroom, off the family room.

"Mom?" I tapped softly on her half-closed door and peered into the dimness.

A dark bundle on the bed shifted. "Rennie?"

My mother, a morning person for as long as I can remember, was still in bed at nine-thirty on a Friday morning. "Are you all right?" I asked, though I knew the answer before the words left my mouth. I walked into her room and turned the dresser light on.

My mother sat up, her short gray hair ruffled from sleeping, and blinked against the light. "I got up a little after six, but I got so tired doing the dishes..."

I gritted my teeth to keep from saying anything. She got tired so easily because she had nothing to distract her from focusing on her every physical twinge, ache or throb. She'd retired a few months ago, after twenty years as the high school secretary. She'd been calling in sick at least once a week for a while and feeling guilty about it, so she finally decided to retire, which was fine. She didn't need the money. My dad's life insurance policy had taken care of that. Except working had helped her concentrate on something else, even if only for a few hours a day. Now, she had all the time in the world to search for odd lumps, bumps and inexplicable bruising, and then she stayed awake all night worrying about it. Last week, something I suspected was trapped gas gave her pain that *had* to be stomach cancer. This week, I'd slipped up and let her watch a movie on Lifetime about a woman overcoming narcolepsy. Less than a day later, she began complaining about unusual sleepy spells.

I popped open the prescription bottle and singled out a pill, confirming the same manufacturer's stamp I always saw. I had to be careful because the labels rarely matched the contents. Hypochondriasis was becoming more widely understood as a genuine medical condition, but there wasn't a lot they could do if a patient refused psychological help. It was a mental illness, disguised by a variety of physical symptoms, both real and exaggerated. For now, the course of treatment had to be the best anti-anxiety drugs money could buy, disguised as whatever cure might be needed this week. No, it wasn't right to trick her, but I'd tried it the other way, telling her the truth, and she'd insisted on going from specialist to specialist, cutting quite a chunk from her savings until I interfered with my co-conspirators Doc Hallacy and Dr. Murphy.

I handed her the pill with the glass of water always on her bedside table. Thus far, she hadn't noticed that most of her prescriptions looked exactly the same though they were for diseases ranging from the obscure to the exotic. I kept track of the bottles for her, hiding them in a locked metal box behind the trashcan in my apartment. I'd started handling her meds last year, after she'd accidentally combined a few pills that weren't meant to be taken together. Drug interaction wasn't my prime concern, but accidental overdose was. You know, a pill for arthritis, a pill for her back, a pill for her narcolepsy—all of them disguised anti-anxiety drugs. That would be bad news.

She started to reach for the pill and then stopped. "Did you wash your hands recently?"

"You mean, in the last thirty seconds or since I did something disgusting?"

"Irene," she said with warning.

I flinched at the sound of my given name. It wasn't something I heard very often—thank goodness—as it was my mother's name too. Rennie might have been an unusual nickname, but it was better than Irene—seriously, is there anybody else under the age of fifty with that name?

"Yes, ma'am. I washed." I could have argued with her about it—the woman wouldn't be satisfied until everyone wore plastic over every inch of exposed skin—but it wasn't worth it, not after the morning I'd had.

She eyed me suspiciously. "I didn't hear the water run."

"You were sleeping," I pointed out.

She just shook her head.

I sighed. "All right, all right. I'll do it again." I set down the water and the pill on her dresser and started for the bedroom door, but her sudden gasp stopped me.

"What," she demanded, "are you wearing?" The tone of her voice sent me immediately back to childhood. I felt six years old again, the age at which I'd decided to learn how the music came out of those eight-track tapes. My mother had busted me pulling the insides out of a John Denver album. The mystery of how the little boxes made music come out remained unsolved, but I'd learned very quickly how to get myself into a whole lot of hot water.

23

I looked down at Bristol's shirt and took a deep breath before facing her. "There was little trouble down at the pharmacy today."

She narrowed her eyes at me. "What kind of trouble ends with you wearing Sheriff Bristol's shirt?" She didn't say the words, *he's married*, but I heard them nonetheless.

"The kind where I get blood on my own shirt and he needs to take it for evidence," I shot back.

Her forehead pinched. "Blood? Why was there blood? Are you all right?" She pushed herself off the bed and came toward me, searching me up and down for obvious open wounds. Worry for her child and the possibility of disease or injury trumped a lecture on morality any day…well, temporarily, at least.

Tucking the sleeve of her robe over her hand to protect herself from my germs, she grasped first my left arm and then my right, turning them to examine the inside of my elbows and wrists, looking for trauma.

I pulled away from her, feeling guilty for manipulating her. "Mom, I'm fine."

"Did those teenagers try to rob Doc again?" She sat down at the foot of her bed, hands clasped together in her lap, probably in a vain attempt to keep herself from poking and prodding at me further.

Early one morning last month, before the Doc's cashier girl had arrived to help at the store, two teenaged boys—identifiable as such by their baggy jeans and the Morrisville High School Track shirt one of them had been wearing—had attempted to steal drugs by trying to slide over the counter and into the back. One had brandished a knife at Doc, obviously hoping to scare him into submission, and the other had carried a pillow case for the goods. Their plan hadn't worked. The boys were no geniuses, and Doc was no fool. He saw them coming—hard to disguise your intent

24

when you're wearing ski masks in the middle of April—and slammed the metal gate down, trapping himself inside with the drugs. Then he called the Sheriff's Office. The boys took off when they found they couldn't get the gate to go up or reach the drugs through the side door. It locked automatically every time it shut, and only the correct code on the keypad above the door handle would open it from the outside.

As far as I knew, Bristol and his folks were still interviewing students to find the master thieves. I didn't think those kids were brave or foolish enough to have done this. Besides, the gate had been up, providing someone a perfect opportunity to shovel everything into a bag and run, but, as I'd told Max, nothing had seemed too much out of place or disturbed. At least, not what you'd expect from a couple of teenage boys trying to rob the place blind.

"I don't think it was robbery this time, Mom." Though that might be a theory worth mentioning to Bristol.

"What happened? Is Doc okay?" My mother frowned.

I hesitated. I didn't want to tell her, but if I didn't, she'd only find out another way. That was the biggest problem of a small town; they had the most efficient information management system I'd ever seen. God help anyone who ever had to buy hemorrhoid cream, a pregnancy test or lactose-free milk. Half the town would know before you even reached the checkout.

"Doc's dead, Mom."

She straightened. "A heart attack." Her hand crept up to the left side of her chest.

"No," I said hastily. "Murder, beaten to death."

She didn't look as though she believed me.

"No natural causes, Mom, I swear." Ever since my dad died of a rare and early heart attack five years ago, the same month I got married, she'd searched herself for every form of disease known to man. She'd always been hyper-aware of her own health, and mine as a child, but my dad's death seemed to have broken something inside her. Like her logic.

She was quiet for a long moment. Then she said, "You found him, didn't you?"

"Yeah." I shrugged. "When the store didn't open right at eight and the lights were still off, I decided to go in and check on him. That's how I ended up with blood on my shirt."

Her mouth pursed. "Irene Mae Harlow, when are you going to learn that no good comes from sticking your nose in other people's business?"

"I thought he might be hurt or need help," I protested.

"You should have just stayed out of it. Called to report it to someone."

"I did. I called Bri…" At her sharp look, I amended myself mid-sentence. "I called the sheriff."

"The sheriff." She didn't sound happy.

"Yeah, Mayor Lottich doesn't really like getting phone calls about dead bodies, Mom."

Slowly, as if her bones pained her, which she probably thought they did, my mother slid off the foot of the bed and moved back toward her pillows piled at the headboard. "You need to get clear of this." She sat down again and, bracing her hands flat on the mattress, boosted herself up and lifted her legs onto the bed.

I started forward to help her, but she waved me away. "I am clear of it," I said. "They know I'm not a suspect. I just have to go in and give a statement so they—"

She shook her head. "I know you, Rennie. You won't be able to leave this alone any more than you did the others."

"I can't help it." The excuse sounded thin even to my own

ears, but true nonetheless. Fact was, people said and did things around me that they would never say or do in front of law enforcement, especially in a murder investigation. If I found out something, I was obligated to make sure it was right before I sent Bristol and his team after it. Besides, Doc Hallacy had helped me out more than I could ever have expected. I had to do something to help. "It's my job to find answers." Well, sort of. Bristol would argue that it was his job to find answers and mine simply to report them.

She sighed. "Rennie, I just want you to be happy, and that'll never happen when you're trying to squeeze in where you don't belong." She looked at me with sorrow and resignation in her eyes. "Jake Bristol's a good man and a good sheriff. He doesn't need your help."

I shifted uncomfortably. My mother was no fool either. "I've got to go, Mom. I have an interview to do and stories to write." I moved closer to her, opened her prescription bottle and tipped a pill into her outstretched hand. She dry-swallowed it rather than risk drinking from the glass of water I'd touched.

"Keep your doors locked," I said. "I'll be back later this afternoon. Just get some rest for now." I turned off the light on the dresser, scooped up the tainted pill—no sense wasting it, I'd put it in one of the other bottles—and started to leave.

"Rennie," she called after me.

"Yeah?"

"Thank you for picking up my medicine again."

Caught by surprise, I felt my heart soften toward her a little. She didn't want to be this way; she just was. "You're welcome, Mom."

"And Rennie?"

"Yeah?"

"Don't forget to change your shirt."

I rolled my eyes. That was more like it.

FOUR

After double checking the lock on my mother's back door, I hurried across the gravel parking area to my apartment over the garage. I was already severely late for my interview with the mayor's wife, though I felt sure the news as to why had already reached her ears and she would therefore be entirely forgiving…in exchange for details of my ordeal, of course. Stopping to change my clothes now would make me later still, but visiting the biggest gossip in town while wearing Bristol's shirt seemed like a bad idea for a lot of reasons, not the least of which was the very real heart attack it would probably give my mother.

I jogged up the wooden stairs on the outer wall of the garage to the single door at the top. The apartment over the garage had been designed in preparation for my grandmother, my father's mother, coming to live with my parents eventually. Only she'd passed away—a brain aneurysm—about three months before my father. It had been a bad year, that one. The space had sat empty until I came home last year.

Two large windows, one on either side of the door, provided the only natural light in the apartment. The door opened into the main room, the only room really. It featured a small kitchenette along the back wall with a breakfast bar to divide it off from the main part of the room, and an even smaller bathroom next to the kitchen. No bedroom, just a pullout couch in the central area.

Fritzy hopped off the couch as soon as I walked in. She paused to stretch, first her back legs and then her front, and her mouth opened in a huge yawn to reveal a long, pink curling tongue.

"Hi, baby," I greeted her. "Did you miss me?"

Her long skinny tail wagged in response. She loped over to my side, limping a little as she always did after napping. Her shoulder, the one with the torn muscle, the reason for her retirement from racing, still bothered her occasionally.

Why people think greyhounds are nervous animals, I will never understand. Spend ten minutes in the company of one, and the greyhound will sleep through about seven of them. They're racers, yeah, but they sprint. Their energy burst is over and done with in about three minutes. Then they sleep for another eighteen hours. They're gorgeous animals—Fritzy is sleek, white with brown spots and a patch of brownish black fur on her right ear— not to mention gentle and intelligent. Yeah, I could be a bit prejudiced. Needless to say Fritzy was a vast improvement over the last creature I'd shared a home with. He had walked on two legs, but he was the real dog.

Fritzy sniffed delicately at the hem of my t-shirt, intrigued by the unfamiliar scent. "Yeah, I know. It's not mine." Unfortunately.

I smoothed the silky fur on the top of her head. It was almost as soft as a rabbit's, ironically enough. I knelt down and rubbed her ears with the back of my knuckles. She groaned in appreciation.

"Mommy's on the run now, but how about a w-a-l-k later, huh?" In conversations with Fritzy, certain words had to be spelled rather than said. She was smart enough to recognize words like treat, riding, walk, and vet, but she didn't quite get the concept of future time. If you say it, you must mean it now, and if you didn't, she'd drive you crazy until you gave in. Too smart for her own good.

I rested the side of my face against her neck, taking a quick moment of comfort in the warmth of her body pressed against my shoulder and chest and the sweet, syrupy smell of her fur.

I'd adopted Fritzy in Chicago before I'd moved, having fallen in love with her at first sight at a neighborhood art fair. One of the greyhound rescue groups had had a booth there. Fritzy had finished racing and needed a home, and I'd needed someone to love me back, my husband having decided that his time was better spent at the office than with me. The second those liquid brown eyes looked up at me, I was lost. I brought her home two weeks later, not bothering to mention our new addition to Jeff. I made bets with myself how long it would take him to notice and object. Jeffrey Michael was not a dog person, and our pristine condo in regentrified (read: can't get a cab after dark) Bucktown probably wasn't the best place for a dog. It turned out not to matter, though, as Jeff wasn't much of a marriage person either, at least not when it came to me.

After one last rub to Fritzy's ears, I headed into the bathroom, which also doubled as my closet, to change my clothes. I took Bristol's t-shirt off, folded it carefully and set it on top of the little four-drawer wicker cabinet that served as my dresser. I'd have to wash the shirt and return it to him…though maybe not right away.

I examined the contents of my closet—an alcove behind the bathroom door, with a bar stretched across it—spending a minute or two I didn't have trying to find something to wear. I'd donated most of my business clothes and everything Jeff had ever given me to wear, including the slutty lingerie I'd never even cut the tags from, almost immediately upon my arrival here. There just wasn't enough room, here, or in my head, for all of it and the memories each piece of fabric would evoke.

Finally, I pulled out a pair of jeans and one of my favorite shirts, a pale blue button down with white pinstripes and white French cuffs. The blue, I knew, would make my eyes look even bluer. The jeans, low rise and boot cut with small back pockets, would create a butt where there wasn't one. Like my chest, my backside tended to disappear in clothing. Not that Mrs. Mayor would appreciate any of this. In fact, if I were being honest with myself, I would have to admit it wasn't really for her benefit. Fortunately, I've discovered lying to me about me can be a very useful habit.

I took another five minutes to run a comb through my disheveled hair and to brush my teeth, both of which would have been done earlier if I hadn't decided to just roll out of bed for what I thought would be a quick trip to the pharmacy. I grimaced, thinking again of what I must have looked like to…everyone at the crime scene.

After a quick goodbye scratch under Fritzy's chin, I collected the contents of my leather bag, which I'd dumped all over the breakfast bar this morning to find my car keys, and headed out, over an hour and fifteen minutes late for my interview at the mayoral mansion.

* * *

The Lottich home wasn't actually a mansion, but it was the biggest house in the Morrisville historical district and the whole town, for that matter. It sat dead center on the Elm Street block, like a queen surrounded by all her attendants. The house resembled an old southern plantation, with a wide veranda, fluffy wedding cake moldings and big white pillars on the front. People always forgot how southern Illinois could be, bumping right up next to Kentucky on the far end as it did. We had a Civil War monument in the town square, and reading it, you could never be quite sure which side it commemorated.

I parked in the side drive, outside the porte cochere, and clattered up the cobblestone walkway. Mrs. Miller, the Lottiches' housekeeper, greeted me at the door and led me inside to the front parlor, just to the left of a magnificent sweeping staircase. I still had never seen the whole house. Mrs. Mayor probably would have shown me if I'd asked, but there was something about a guided tour that took the magic out of old places like these.

"Good morning, Rennie, dear," Gloria Lottich called to me with barely repressed eagerness in her voice, as I walked into the parlor. She didn't bother to get up from the throne of her high-backed wing chair. "Is everything all right? I was starting to worry."

I resisted the urge to roll my eyes. Oh, please, someone had been on the phone to her ten seconds after I hung up with Bristol. If I played this right, I might get a few leads on something other than the best place to buy tulip bulbs.

Taking my seat in the chair across from her, I felt as I always did—that I should have curtsied first. "I'm sorry for the delay, Mrs. Lottich. I should have called but..." Honestly, I had no excuse for not calling her, other than the truth. She would have kept me on the phone for hours and still expected me to come over. But I couldn't say *that*.

"Oh, don't trouble yourself about that, dear. How *are* you?" Her sharp eyes, slightly distorted by the strength of her glasses, honed in on me, searching for any signs of distress that she could later report. The frames of her glasses matched the exact shade of her orchid double-knit suit. I'd never seen Mrs. Mayor in anything other than her Sunday best. Though, I wondered if that phrase still had meaning if someone dressed that way every day.

Today was no exception. All she was missing was a pillbox hat with a little veil, and dollars to doughnuts, it was sitting upstairs on the bed with her purse. She was roughly the same age as my mother, but the way she dressed always made me think she was older. Not that she'd be pleased to hear that. Not that I'd ever

33

be foolish enough to say it.

I gritted my teeth. In truth, finding Doc Hallacy's body was the last thing I wanted to talk about with her, but I knew she wouldn't let it go until I offered up something. "I don't know if you've heard," I said with fake hesitation. Oh, how I hated playing this game. "But something awful happened this morning."

The artificial build-up of suspense had Mrs. Mayor practically leaning over the tea table between us to catch my next words.

"I'm afraid Doc Hallacy...has passed. I found him this morning at the pharmacy."

For someone who'd been dealing with this news nearly as long as I had, she gave a fair imitation of shock. She straightened up in her chair. Her eyes went wide, and she blinked rapidly. "Oh, my dear Lord. That's terrible."

"Yes." If she wanted more, she'd have to drag it from me.

This suited Gloria just fine. She was more than willing to interrogate. "What happened? Was it murder? How did he look?"

I repeated the same story I'd told Bristol, essentially, leaving out, to Gloria's disappointment, a detailed description of poor Doc's corpse. I also kept quiet about hearing the back door to the pharmacy open and shut. I didn't know if Bristol wanted that revealed. If I mentioned it to Gloria, not only would the whole town know in under six minutes, but there would suddenly be rumors about who I might have seen fleeing the scene, even though I'd been running too fast in the opposite direction to see anybody.

"What does Sheriff Bristol say? Does he have any suspects?" She poured tea from a small silver teapot into two dainty china cups. Her pinky finger, of course, stood out at a right angle as she did.

For once I was grateful for Bristol's unwillingness to share information with the press. I shook my head. "Honestly, I don't know. If he's got any theories, he didn't share them with me." Yet. I fully expected to pry them out of him at our appointment this afternoon.

Her brow furrowed in disappointment—foiled again—before she lit upon another idea and her smile returned. "But surely you must have some hint of what truly happened. After all, you're the one who tracked down that nasty man who killed Coach Swenson."

Ah, flattery. It would get her absolutely nowhere this time, considering she probably had as much information as I did. I took the opportunity to redirect her. "Mrs. Mayor...I mean, Mrs. Lottich..."

She beamed at my not-so-subtle mistake. She loved being reminded of her husband's office and associated with its honor by proxy, though she would be quick to deny it if asked.

"Max has asked me to write the tribute article for Doc Hallacy, and I was hoping you could give me some advice." It'd occurred to me that the head of the rumor mill herself might be just the person to point fingers and name names when it came to possibilities for Doc's killer. Not that I could approach it that directly. "I'd like to talk to some of Doc's friends and family for the article, if they're willing. Who would you recommend?"

She immediately sat forward in her chair. The only thing Gloria Lottich loved more than gossip was giving her opinion, especially when solicited as an expert. "Well," she pursed her lips in thought, "You know, Ginjer Buchanan is his only relative left in town, a grand-niece, I think. And as for his friends..." She shook her head, tssking in the back of her throat. "Most of them have moved on."

I paused in the midst of digging a pen and notebook out of my bag. "You mean died?"

"No, Rennie, of course not." She sounded offended. "They're in Florida or Arizona, warm places. Though I suppose some have likely passed on altogether." Her brow furrowed, and I knew she had yet more to give. "There's the Sturgeon girl who worked part-time for him at the register. I can never remember which one. They all look the same to me." *Like their drunk and disorderly father.* The words were made clear by the disdain in her voice.

Then she brightened. "You might try Marty Halpern, if he's willing to talk to you. He and Doc were friends from way back to their elementary school days, alphabetical order you know, until they had a falling out some time ago."

A falling out was always good, particularly when looking for a murderer with a motive. "What did they fight about?"

She leaned a little closer as though she were afraid Mrs. Wilson, laboring way back in the kitchen, might hear. "No one really knows, though there were rumors that it might have been over Maybelle." She whispered the name, and then crossed herself.

Maybelle Hallacy had been Doc's wife for forty plus years until she'd died a few years back. I didn't live here at the time, so I couldn't remember if there'd been anything odd about her death. I made a note to look it up in back issues of the *Gazette*. Max might also know—that had been about the time he'd shown up here.

"Is there anyone I should avoid? People who might have some not so nice things to say about Doc?" I tried to sound casual.

"Well, Kitty Alexander was never too fond of him. The two of them were always battling over parking spaces on First Street."

Kitty's Collectibles sat kitty-corner from Doc's pharmacy on the other corner of Main and First. I'd tried once in high school to go in there to buy a gift for Mother's Day, but the stench of potpourri combined with the claustrophobic feeling caused by lace draped, stapled and hot glued to every available surface drove me

36

right back out into the street. Kitty was probably happier without high school students patronizing her store anyway. Apparently somebody shopped there, though. It was still in business, had been for as long as I could remember, and was doing well enough to provoke Kitty into arguing over parking with Doc. Still, parking spaces weren't exactly what I had in mind.

"Anyone with a grudge?" I tried again.

"Why, no. Doc didn't have any enemies. You should know that, Rennie. The man never turned a single person wrong his whole life." Gloria's mouth started to turn down, signaling my window was starting to close.

"Not even by accident? The wrong meds in the wrong bottle?" I squeezed in one last question.

"Rennie Harlow, that's enough out of you, disparaging the dead." She glared at me and crossed herself again, an odd contradiction to see. "You let the sheriff and his deputies ask all the questions, they know what they're doing. It's...unseemly for you to be involved." Because I was a divorced woman? Because I wasn't a cop? Interesting how her opinion of me shifted once she realized I had nothing left to tell her.

"Yes, Ma'am." I ducked my head, attempting to look sufficiently shamed. If I didn't, she'd call my mother. No lie.

"So, I hear you have some spectacular tulips for show this year." I changed the subject to one guaranteed to distract Gloria from her ire.

She perked up immediately. "Oh, yes. Margene Bristol has worked miracles with hers. As for mine, well, you'll just have to see them to believe them." She paused, narrowing her eyes at me. "There are going to be photos with this article, yes? Last year, there weren't any photos and we can't have that catastrophe again. If I need to call Mr. Biddleman again to make it happen, I will."

I hastened to reassure her that Johnny Mac, our young (read: unpaid) photographer, would be out with his camera later, per our previous arrangements. That seemed to pacify her temporarily. Now if I could just keep her away from the fertilizer versus compost debate that had kept me here for half a day last year, I'd be all set.

***

An hour and a half later, I managed to escape Mrs. Mayor, knowing much more about worm poo, the essential ingredient in vermi-composting, than any sane person should. Before heading to the Sheriff's Office or the *Gazette*, both on my list for this afternoon, I decided to stop by Ginjer Buchanan's. If Mrs. Mayor was right about her address—trust me, she would be—Ginjer's place was on the way, sort of, and she might have something she'd like to say for the article about her great-uncle.

"He was a lying, thieving bastard." Ginjer, a short red-head—apparently her parents had suffered from a severe lack of imagination—stood in her doorway, glaring up at me. She was a few years older than I, enough that I'd never had occasion to know her. Based on ten seconds of her company, I wasn't sure I wanted to.

I managed a relatively calm, "Oh, really?"

"He cut me and Byron out of his will."

"When was that?" I asked casually. I hoped anger would keep her tongue loose and her brain pre-occupied, so she'd keep talking without wondering what right I had to know all this.

"Couple months ago. Left just enough for us to bury him and some for Junior's college fund." She jerked her head back toward the house, I guess to indicate that the loud squalling coming from inside was the college-bound Junior, in eighteen years or so.

"Did he say why?" My fingers itched to haul out a pencil and

38

start scribbling notes, but I thought she might get suspicious of me taking notes on Doc Hallacy's will for what was supposed to be a tribute article.

"No. Just said he felt the money wasn't his no more once he died and it should go back to the one who gave it to him."

I stepped forward, instantly more alert. Can anyone say motive? "Who?" Oh, good, Rennie. Very subtle.

She pursed her mouth, her eyes narrowing. "What kind of article did you say you was writing?"

Uh-oh. Time to backpedal. "A tribute article. Do you have anything you'd like me to include about your great-uncle?"

She smirked. "Yeah. He wasn't so great." With that she let the screen door slam and disappeared inside.

Walking back to my car, parked on the street, I pondered Ginjer's words. He wasn't so great…because he'd taken away money she'd considered hers. Or was there more to it? I looked mournfully back at the little crackerbox brick house, and the potential answers still inside with Ginjer. Bristol would have to take it from here; Ginjer wouldn't be openly confessing anything to me anymore.

At least I could rule her out, probably, for Hallacy's murder, I thought, as I got back into my car. She'd known months ago she was getting cut out of the will. If she'd been enraged about it to the point of murder, she'd have done something then. Killing him now would have no benefit.

No money, at least, I corrected myself as I headed back toward the center of town. It might have put her in a better mood. Generally that was not enough to push someone to murder, though. I'd read once where someone said all murders are motivated by just one thing. Unfortunately, I couldn't remember the one thing. In my limited experience, murder was motivated by money, sex, or fear. Clearly Ginjer Buchanan was out, at least on the money factor, but I'd have dearly loved to know who the mysterious beneficiary of Doc Hallacy's will was.

FIVE

I pulled into a parking space in front of the *Gazette* at about quarter to one. Stomach growling, I stopped to pick up a BLT at Ruby's Cafe before heading next door to see Max.

"Hey, I'm here." I dropped my bag and sandwich on my cluttered desk. It wasn't really *my* desk, just a spare. I'd found I took deadlines a lot more seriously with Max breathing down my neck. Quite productive really. In my old life, I'd been a marketing writer for a national bank. Water eroded rocks faster than projects were completed there. Working freelance for a daily newspaper, and Max, had cured me of that luxury.

I booted up my computer and swiveled to face Max as he emerged from his office in the back, papers in hand.

"Bristol's already called twice looking for you." Max didn't even look up from the copy he scowled at. "Lie or lay?"

"Like someone taking a nap or setting something down?" I asked without pausing. "What did he want?"

"Taking a nap," Max said. "Your statement and a preview of the stories we plan to run on the Hallacy murder, which he will *not* be getting." He looked up long enough to glare at me.

"Lie," I answered his original question and ignored the rest, knowing it would only lead to a fight.

"Good girl." Max apparently counted my silence as consent on that particular matter. "There's a pile of stuff for you." He tilted his head to the desk right in front of the door that had served as the receptionist's desk, when the *Gazette* had had one. "People have been dropping off submissions for the tribute all morning."

I got up and grabbed the stack of envelopes, notes and even a folded drink napkin and took them back to my desk. People were encouraged to submit their memories of the deceased. To be included in the article had become a major badge of honor, to the point where I'd had occasion to wonder if people were just making things up.

I started going through the pile, not surprised to find all the stories of Doc Hallacy's kindness. Prescriptions given at half-price or free for those who needed them, but had no money or insurance. His large donations of time and money over at the animal shelter. His role in the Christmas parade as Santa's tallest and oldest living elf, something the kids always got a kick out of for some strange reason. I remembered, as child, being fascinated by the idea that an elf could be as tall as my dad.

I sorted all the contributions into those I would use and those that said the same thing only not as well, surprised to find my eyes welling at the kind of schlock I normally rolled them at. Then again, I didn't usually find my tributees dead, did I? At least, not most of the time.

"Deadline, deadline." Max buzzed by my chair, piles of invoices in his hand.

"Yeah, I got it." I pulled myself together. There'd be time for grieving after I was done.

Three hours later, I sent both articles to the laser jet printer on the other side of my desk and pushed back from my computer, rubbing ineffectually at the tightness in my neck and shoulders. Recounting this morning's events in a calm and logical manner had taken more out of me than I'd realized. Writing the tribute article had nearly finished me off. After coming close to tears multiple times, I just wanted to go home and curl into a ball.

"The discovery story and the tribute for Eugene Hallacy are

ready," I called back toward Max's office. I'd realized in writing the tribute that I hadn't even known Doc's first name.

Max scooped my printouts off the printer, red pencil in hand. After a few long minutes, he grunted. "Your headlines are shit, as usual, but the rest is passable."

I rolled my eyes. "Gee, thanks. I'm all fluttery inside." Typical Max. He never admitted to liking of any of my stuff, fearing I'd press my case for full-time employment, yet he rarely made more than a few minor changes.

I printed a second copy of both pieces for Bristol, stood up and slung my bag over my shoulder. "Can you live without me for an hour or so?"

Max looked up long enough to glare at me and the papers in my hands. "It's called freedom of the press, Rennie. The sheriff does not have the right to review—"

"It's the only way he'll let us run something, Max, you know that," I said.

"He does not have editorial control over this paper. I do."

"Yeah, and unless you want all your future stories about Morrisville murder, sex and mayhem to include giant blanks where the details would be, you better let him look these over," I said. "We can't afford to lose the Sheriff's Office as a source."

"Whose side are you on?" he demanded.

I refused to back down. "Mine. It's up to you and Bristol to work out the rest."

After staring at me for a long moment, Max shook his head and muttered something about working in a police state, before turning and stalking back to his office.

I sighed and headed for the door.

"If he tries to cut too much, I'm running it in original form," Max shouted.

I waved to him without looking back. "Bye, Max."

***

As usual, the trip to the Sheriff's Office took all of about ten minutes, even with traffic. If you could call three cars and a combine traffic. I pulled into the parking lot, feeling my stomach flutter with an excited nervousness.

"That's trouble, Ren," I muttered. "More trouble you don't need." I couldn't help it, though, any more than I could help finding Doc this morning. Only this was a tragedy entirely of my own making.

I took a deep breath, gathered all of my stuff and got out of the car. As I walked toward the building, shuffling pages to get the articles in order for Bristol, I nearly collided with a woman just outside the door to the office.

I stopped short, but my forward momentum almost carried me into her anyway. "Sorry." I smiled so she'd know it wasn't deliberate.

The woman, young woman really, not much more than a girl, looked up at me with red-rimmed eyes. "It's all right." Then she shuffled to one side to get around me.

Recognition slid over me. "Hey, wait."

The girl paused, turning to look over her shoulder at me. Her dark hair bounced in a high pony tail. She looked like any young high school or college student. Except her blue cardigan had gone to thread at the elbows, revealing the white of her skin beneath, and her jeans were well-worn and patched, albeit very carefully, across the knee. Who patched jeans anymore? One of twelve Sturgeon girls wearing cast-offs, I guessed.

I stepped a little closer, still juggling my bag, papers and car keys. "You're one of the...I mean, you worked for Doc Hallacy right?"

44

She nodded, her eyes growing bright with tears. "Through high school and between classes now." Hiccups broke her sentence into fragments.

One of the Sturgeon girls made it into college? I barely kept myself from asking the question out loud. Then I remembered that one of the youngest girls had been rumored to be beyond-Sturgeon smart. Was it Jamie, Julie...or maybe Jenny?

"Jenny?" I hazarded a guess.

She nodded again.

I let out a silent breath of relief at my correct guess. For obvious reasons, the Sturgeons were famously ill-tempered when confused for another sibling. "I'm Rennie Harlow. I—"

"I know who you are. Your mama is Mrs. Harlow."

I pulled back a little, startled. "Yeah. How did you know?"

She shrugged. "Doc Hallacy sometimes used to tell me about people."

I raised my eyebrows. Most of that information was confidential...

"Oh, he didn't say names or anything," she added hastily. A slight blush rose in her cheeks. "Just the circumstances. I put it together when I saw you coming in all the time."

And Doc was lonely with no one else to talk to, I translated silently.

She sighed deeply. "I think Doc missed his wife." She lifted her eyes to mine. "Did you know Mrs. Hallacy?"

I nodded. "She ordered books for me when I was a kid."

"Yeah. She was nice that way." A tear spilled down her cheek. "But now they're both gone." Jenny started to move past me.

"Wait. I'm writing a story, a follow-up to the tribute article I'm working on." A little fib, but not much of one, considering. "Can you tell me if there was anything out of the ordinary the last few days? Was Doc upset about anything?"

She sniffled, wiped her face with her sleeve, and then shook her head. "Not that I know of. But I was only there for a few hours a day, after my eight o'clock class and until five, so I'd have time to get back over to the community college in Litchfield for my evening class. I could have come in more, but he…he wanted me to keep going to school." A wan smile pulled her mouth. "He said he liked the peace and quiet of the store to himself sometimes."

I nodded, trying to rein in my impatience. She was grieving. I was too, but somehow, on the trail to possible murderer information, that emotion got blindsided by plain-old eagerness. "What about anyone else? Anyone come to the store, acting bent out of shape?"

She started to shake her head and then stopped. Her head snapped up, and I could see a sudden wildness in her eyes.

My pulse jumped. "What is it?"

She shook her head again, rapidly this time. "No, no. I…I have to go." She turned on her heel and half-ran through the parking lot to a beat up Chevy pick-up in the corner.

"Jenny," I called out after her. She didn't so much as pause. The girl knew something, but she wasn't going to pass it along to me, not willingly. That meant I'd have to tell Bristol, if he hadn't already made the same realization about Jenny. I grimaced. Whenever possible, I preferred bringing him answers, rather than more questions. He probably had enough of those on his own.

SIX

"Well, what do you know? It's Rennie, our very own cadaver dog. Maybe we should call you Ren-tin-tin...get it?" Deputy George Barnes, taking his shift at the reception desk in the Sheriff's Office, snorted with laughter at his own joke. Larger departments often used trained dogs for search and rescue or recovery missions. Morrisville had little money and even less need for such a thing. Though, I suppose with my arrival I'd filled the role well enough, albeit unintentionally.

I blew Barnes a kiss, leaving my middle finger up a second longer than all the others, which only made him laugh harder. I liked him even though he drove me crazy sometimes. Barnes was the most senior member of the Morrisville Sheriff's Office. He'd busted beer parties back when I was in high school. He'd had no interest in the sheriff's position when it opened up two years ago. Hated politics, he said. Bristol had stepped up and won the election, while Barnes remained where he was, seemingly content. Barnes looked to me like all cops should: big, broad-shouldered, hair in a buzz cut, a little red-faced, and no matter what the temperament, a certain hardness in the eyes. The look that says I have seen more than you have imagined on your worst day. He was married, for twenty-seven years now, to the same woman. They had three or four kids and were expecting their first grandchild any day. The highlight of his day was teasing me, a favor I returned with equal enthusiasm.

I made a face at him. "Go choke on a doughnut." Around here it was far more likely to be a bran muffin these days, much to

47

everyone's dismay. Sheryl, the only woman on the force, was on a health food kick.

Barnes waved me on, and I pushed past the gate into the central area of the office. Dented file cabinets, in varying shades of olive green and dirty beige, lined the perimeter. Frosted windows, set too high up in the walls to be considered for escape, let in a good amount of late afternoon sunshine, making dust motes in the air glow like microscopic bits of diamond. Four desks with fake wood surfaces and metal drawers, purchased at an auction when two small country high schools merged last year, were stationed at various points in the room.

The room buzzed with a surprising amount of activity today, unlike most other afternoons. Laura Radnor's three children swarmed all over Deputy Trent Sheffey's desk, while their mother sat in a visitor's chair and attempted to maneuver her yet again pregnant belly, covered in a well-worn maternity tunic, into a more comfortable position. Sheffey was on the phone, but watched the children with distinct dismay as their dirty fingers touched everything within their reach. He didn't have kids, or even a wife, let alone a girlfriend, so he wasn't used to the destructive ways of bored children.

Sheffey was younger than me, probably in his late twenties, and he looked more like a persnickety math teacher than a deputy. He had a slight build and stood only an inch or so taller than my five foot seven. He wore wire-rimmed glasses and a pristine uniform, and he probably spent hours trying to comb the wave in his sandy blonde hair into submission. Sheffey liked everything to be in order, for everything to proceed as expected, for all rules to be obeyed. It's one of the things that made him a good cop, in my opinion. Although in my limited experience, law enforcement rarely went exactly the way it was supposed to, which meant

Sheffey occasionally had some bad days, this probably being one of them. I could practically see his hands twitching to remove the Radnor children bodily from his desk and begin wiping down every surface.

On the other side of the room, Ginjer Buchanan waited with a sullen-looking, overweight man in a plaid shirt, probably her husband, Byron. They sat in the visitor chairs in front of the desk that had been occupied by Deputy Andrews until he retired and moved to Florida last month. Bristol was in the process of trying to find a replacement for him, too. From the sheer bustle of this place, I'd say he needed it. Though short of the Foundation Festival, a town carnival that always sounded to me like a celebration of women's undergarments instead of a commemoration of Morrisville's beginnings, murder was the only thing that could generate this kind of energy.

Barnes's desk, toward the middle of the room, was empty because he was up front, but it was readily identifiable by the fast food wrappers littering the surface. Sheryl wasn't at her desk, next to Barnes', either. She was probably answering a call or off-duty.

Bristol's office was in the back. The door was closed, but through the windows I could see him on the phone, so I hung back for a couple minutes.

To my left, I heard Sheffey tell Laura Radnor, "Ma'am, I'm sorry, but we can't let you into the pharmacy."

"But I need those pills," she said. Large blotches of red blossomed on her face.

"I called the pharmacy over at the hospital, and they said they're willing to fill your prescription for you, provided Dr. Murphy will verify it for you."

"You don't understand." Laura's brown eyes, dark circles under them, brimmed suddenly with tears. "It's not the same." She bent her head into her hands and sobbed. Her thin dark hair, pulled up with a faded blue scrunchie, bobbed as her shoulders shook.

I thought of the pill bottle Bristol had taken out of the pharmacy for me and felt a sharp pang of guilt.

"Excuse me, Laura?" I received a relieved look from Sheffey as my reward for intervening. "Can I pick something up for you or…" I swallowed hard and Sheffey winced, as one of her boys located the pencil sharpener, opened it, and dumped the shavings all over his own head. "…maybe keep an eye on the kids so you can run over to the hospital?"

She lifted her head from her hands long enough to look up at me, a slight frown on her face.

"I'm Rennie Harlow. I used to live here, but I left and then—"

"I know who you are." She rose to her feet with a swaying motion. Her frown grew deeper, her mouth pursing in displeasure. "You're the one who found Doc Hallacy dead."

"Um, yeah, I did," I responded, startled by her animosity. "But—"

"You can just keep your favors, Rennie Harlow. I don't need 'em. Nobody does. Come on kids, let's go." With one last glare at me, Laura Radnor scooped her purse and diaper bag off the chair and started toward the door, a small parade of children following behind her, the youngest trailing pencil shavings and graphite dust in his wake.

"But I didn't kill him." I stared after her. I didn't know Laura very well, so I had no idea what I'd done to offend her. She lived out in one of the trailers at the edge of town. She'd moved here from Carlinville after I'd left twelve years ago. I only knew her because I'd seen her in here a few times—bailing out her bar-fighting husband usually—and I'd asked Sheryl who she was.

"Sometimes finding the victim is close enough." Bristol's

deep voice sounded behind me, making me jump. "As it is, Laura's been having a hard time keeping everything together since her husband tore up his leg working at Smithery." J.T. Smithery was a propane factory, one of the biggest employers in town.

I turned and saw Bristol standing too close for my own comfort. Sometimes I worried I might reach out and touch him without realizing what I'd done until it was too late.

Taking a big step backward, I nearly collided with Sheffey, who'd found a broom and dustpan somewhere and was now busily sweeping up after the Radnor tornado.

Bristol frowned at me. "You all right, Rennie?"

"No more messed up than usual," I muttered.

A smile flickered across Bristol's mouth before vanishing under the weight of his normal somber expression. He held his arm out, directing me to his office.

I sat down in the chair across from his desk, and he closed the door. The sudden silence surrounding us made me nervous again, not that anything would happen. I tried to resist the urge to babble and failed.

"Hey, did you know Ginjer out there," I jerked my thumb back toward the other room, "got cut out of her Great-Uncle Eugene Hallacy's will? She's not too happy about it either. Seems some mysterious beneficiary got what she considered her share of the dough." I jounced my foot on the floor, unable to keep still.

Bristol dropped into the cracked leather chair behind his desk and leveled an exasperated look at me. "They haven't read Hallacy's will yet."

"Yeah, I know." I grinned, pleased at having intrigued him.

He sighed, rubbing his face. "All right. I give. How do you know about the will?"

"Ginjer told me. We had a real heart to heart."

"Am I going to be getting another complaint about someone impersonating a deputy again?"

"No," I said, a little hurt. "For the record, I never told that guy I was a cop. He assumed it, and I didn't correct it. A rookie mistake, but you caught him, didn't you?"

"He almost killed you first, but yeah, we got him." Bristol shook his head, his mouth tight with disapproval.

I shrugged. Coach Swenson's murderer, Ritchie Larson, a big time drug dealer from Litchfield, had come after me when I wrote a story claiming one freelance reporter had figured out who *dunnit* based on some key evidence at the scene. I'd had Bristol's permission to write the story, just not to sneak into the school natatorium where I ended up confronting Larson and lying, sort of, about my exact role in law enforcement. It had worked out okay in the end. Bristol figured out Larson had gotten past the surveillance detail on his apartment and where he was headed. He showed up just in time to save me from going out with a big splash.

"All right," he said. "Let's see what you've got on this one."

I handed him the tribute article as well as the story I'd written about the discovery this morning.

After a few minutes of reading, he looked up to give me an admonishing frown. "I said *don't* mention the cane. We need to be able to eliminate any false confessions we might get."

I sighed. "Max'll love that. Are there really that many people waiting around to confess to a murder they didn't commit so they can go to jail for the rest of their lives?"

"You'd be surprised." Then he went back to reading.

After a moment, he shook his head. "Beaten to death? No."

"That's what it looked like to me."

"Preliminary report from the county coroner says it was single blow to the back of the head that killed him."

"And the rest?" I flinched, remembering Doc Hallacy's bloodied face staring up at me.

He shrugged. "Icing."

I made a face at his choice of words.

"So, uh, I guess it would have to be a pretty strong man to kill him with just one hit?" I asked, as casually as I could.

Bristol scowled at me. "Forget it, Rennie. I'm not sharing suspect information with you."

I pounced. "Then you have a suspect or suspects in mind?"

He groaned and leaned forward in his chair, resting his elbows on his desk, his warm brown eyes steady on mine. "You are enough to try a man, Rennie."

He meant it innocently enough, but somehow the combination of those words—hello, try is exactly what I'd like to do—in that magnificent voice and the intensity of his look sent heat crawling up my neck.

Abruptly he looked away. "Your statement."

"Uh, yeah." I busied myself with searching for something, anything in my bag. *Great job, Rennie. How about just announcing, hey Bristol, I know you're married and all, but I'm nearly drowning in lust over here. Can you give a girl a hand?*

"Start from the beginning. You went to the pharmacy to pick up your mother's prescription," he prompted.

"Yeah, and I got there a little before eight, but I didn't try to go in. You know how Doc Hallacy is...was." I grimaced at the slip. "Exactly eight A.M. to six P.M., no more, no less."

He nodded a silent encouragement to continue.

"So I waited for a few minutes, and then when it got to be past eight and he hadn't come to the front door to open it up or flip over the sign, I got a weird feeling."

"At which point you should have called us," Bristol

53

interjected.

"Right." I mimed holding a phone to my ear. "Hello, Sheriff? I have this creepy feeling, and I want you to drop everything and come investigate."

"A call like that from you Rennie, and you're damn right we'll come investigate."

"Well, I didn't want to waste your time." I tried not to sound defensive.

He waved his hand for me to continue.

"When I stepped up to the door to look in, I noticed the lights were still off and then the door just sort of opened."

He raised his eyebrows at me, tipping his head forward in an I-know-better look. "You mean, it was unlocked and you decided to poke your head in? Or it was actually standing open?"

I stuck my tongue out at him. "Neither, wise guy. It was…" I thought for a moment. "Shut, but not snapped closed. Like someone had shut the door without checking to make sure it clicked into place."

"Or, like he was expecting someone."

"You mean he was meeting someone before the pharmacy opened? What makes you think that?" I narrowed my eyes at him. "What do you know that you're not telling?" An idea jolted me upright in my seat. "Did you get something off the security cameras?"

"They're on a timer, starting at eight A.M. exactly and focused only on the main door. The only thing we have is you, entering and exiting the pharmacy."

"So at least you know I'm telling you the truth," I said, a tiny part of me relieved. Having been a suspect once, I found myself much more aware of being caught in that situation again. "But you know something about Doc meeting someone?" I pressed.

He shrugged. "Just exploring possibilities. Keep going." He remained maddeningly silent on what was running through his head.

I exhaled loudly in frustration. "I walked in, smelled the smell—"

"Smell?" he asked.

I frowned at him. "You know...the smell." The smell of someone dying or recently dead is not something you easily forget. Not decomposition, not yet, but the coppery scent of blood and the foul stench of bowels and bladder released at the moment of death. No one ever talks about it on TV or in the movies. Even now, months after finding assistant Coach Swenson, I couldn't go anywhere near a pool without smelling the chlorine and remembering it with that underlying heavier, fleshier odor.

"Also a good time to have left and called us," Bristol pointed out.

I exhaled loudly in exasperation. "If he were just badly injured, he might have needed help. And I didn't want to cause a fuss in case I was wrong."

"You're right, though. You can't mistake that smell."

I nodded.

"So you headed toward the counter in the back. Did you notice anything out of place back there?"

Doc stuffed under the counter, I thought about saying, but I didn't. I tried to remember exactly what I might have seen. "It was so dark back there, just a little light coming through that tiny, high-up-there window in the back wall. The metal gate was up obviously. And... oh!" I stopped, realizing something I'd forgotten until just now. "The side door, you know the one that leads into the storage area and then out the back—it was open."

"Wedged, actually, with pad of paper. Otherwise, it closes

automatically."

I nodded slowly, piecing it together. "They used the side door to get out the back delivery door." That made sense. I'd heard the heavy door banging shut. "That means the murderer hung around for a bit after killing Doc, or maybe even left with the intention to come back." I shuddered.

"Or, it means that Doc knew who killed him and propped the door open himself to let him or her in."

"No." I shook my head. "He never let anyone back there, not even Maybelle when she was alive."

"But there are no signs of a struggle. If someone had jumped the counter like you did, I don't think Doc would have taken it lying down."

I winced, remembering Doc on the floor.

"No pun intended." Bristol lifted his hand up to stop my protest.

I nodded.

"So anything else?"

I thought about it for a long moment, and then shook my head. "Sorry."

"It's all right," he said. "Just let me know if you remember anything else." He bent his head over the papers on his desk, scrawling some notes.

I reached for my bag and hesitated, uncertain if that was a dismissal or not. Usually they read back your statement and have you sign it but...

"I noticed you got your window fixed," he said without looking up.

The BMW's rear side window had been broken out by Ritchie Larson before he'd moved on to bigger and more potentially fatal scare tactics. I'd refused to get it fixed for a month or so, intending to ship the broken bits back to Jeff in Chicago. The first pieces of his beloved car that I hoped to send. On principle, I'd left the window opening covered in plastic and tape, just as I avoided most oil changes and all routine maintenance that didn't directly affect the car's drivability. I refused to sink another penny into that mid-life crisis on wheels.

Until Bristol cornered me one day inside the *Gazette* office with Max gone.

"Get it fixed, Rennie. It's dangerous. Anyone has access to your car and you, when you're it," he'd said.

I'd waved off his concern. "You caught him already. No big deal."

"With you there'll probably be another one. Someone skimming out of the pension fund at Smithery or something. You'll find out, start investigating, and they'll come gunning for you."

I'd rolled my eyes. "Bristol, I told you—"

"Damnit, Rennie. Just get it fixed." He had leaned over my desk, hands fisted on the surface. "I don't want to be answering a call to come get your body."

I'd looked up then and seen the fear for me in his eyes and in the way lines formed by his mouth when he frowned deeply. Something tight had loosened in my chest, setting free a flood of warmth that buoyed me for days. So I'd agreed to fix the window.

"Yeah." I felt the heat return to my face, remembering that moment between us. "Bob over at the Marathon did it for me. He runs a glass shop too."

Bristol brought his gaze up from the papers to my face again. I struggled not to fidget or blush again under that scrutiny. "Good," he said finally. "Glad to hear it."

My heart thudded loudly in my chest, so much so I could hear it. "Listen, Bristol, I wanted to—"

"Oh, no, Deputy Barnes, I'll just go ahead and go in." The familiar voice reached my ears through the closed door. Bristol's mouth tightened.

A second later, Margene Bristol pushed open the office door. Her sweeping gaze caught me first, and I struggled not to sit back in my chair, like four feet and a desk between me and her husband wasn't enough.

She strode in, carrying a large paper grocery bag, and stopped directly in front of her husband, keeping her back to me. Today she wore a bright pink sweater set over a long denim skirt, conservative sheriff's wife for sure. On Margene, though, those clothes never quite fit right, more like a costume she desperately wanted to make her own. The scoop neck tank beneath the cardigan scooped a little too low, revealing more than a hint of her formidable curves. In the kindergarten-teacher denim skirt, she managed to flash those man-catching legs through slits on both sides. Even her hair, a sleek shoulder-length bob, seemed out of place with her rounded face.

Not that I am one to criticize style. The short, trendy haircut I'd loved in the city had started to grow out rather unevenly, due to my fear of new hair stylists, and my desire to dress up had disappeared with my relocation to the capital of cowboy boots and overalls.

"Genie, what are you doing here?" Bristol's tone was even, but not pleased. Or, at least it seemed that way to me.

"I heard about poor Doc Hallacy and I thought you might like something to eat. I guessed you wouldn't be making it home for dinner," Margene said. I knew she was fighting the urge to look over at me.

"That was nice of you." Bristol rubbed his hand over his face.

"But we're sort of in the middle of something right now."

Then she did turn to look at me. "Rennie."

"Margene," I said.

"I'm sorry, but I didn't pack enough for two." She set the grocery bag on Bristol's desk. "I had no idea you might be here."

That was a lie. If she'd heard about Doc, I'd bet money it went something like this, 'Rennie Harlow found Doc Hallacy dead this morning.' Whatever. "That's all right. I'm on my way out of here anyway." I started to rise.

"In just a minute," Bristol said. "I've got a couple more things to go over with you."

I sat back down, feeling a bit like a chew toy caught between a pair of opposing Dobermans.

"Jake, honey, before I head back home, would you mind checking that right front tire again? I have to go pick up Chelsea from the Thoreau's." She gave him a sweet smile, revealing almost perfect teeth—the two front ones overlapped a little.

Deep lines appeared on either side of his mouth, but he nodded and got up from behind his desk. He left the door open, clearly expecting Margene to follow, as was I. I didn't think her front tire was low any more than I thought her appearance here was coincidental. Her request was a demonstration of territory—*My man, stay away.* Apparently, that wasn't the only one she was prepared to make.

She hung back in the office, waiting until Bristol had walked far enough away not to hear, or not to hear much.

"You've been here a lot lately, Rennie." She leaned against his desk, attempting a casual posture ruined by the tension in her shoulders and her straight-as-a-ruler back.

"Only when something bad happens." I jounced my leg on the floor again, wondering if I could bolt for the door. This little bit of girl talk was already making me uncomfortable.

"Which seems to be fairly often with you. Why do you suppose that is?" She smiled sweetly at me, but her eyes remained cold.

"I don't know." Let's see, thirty seconds to walk out the door, ten seconds to find her mini-van in the parking lot. Another thirty seconds, maybe even a minute to look at the tire…I was going to be stuck here for at least another minute and a half.

She crossed her arms over her chest, making sure that her engagement and wedding rings were clearly visible on the hand resting on her sweater sleeve. "Some would say that certain people look for trouble because they want the attention. That doesn't seem quite fair, does it? Taking attention from those who should rightfully have it?"

Come on, Bristol. Hurry up! "I don't know, Margene." I resisted the urge to look over my shoulder through the window overlooking the rest of the office, to see if he was returning. I was terrible at these clouded and coded girl conversations; high school had taught me that. I knew exactly what she was getting at, but I had no idea how to respond. Being too direct would cause offense and probably pseudo-hurt feelings. Not responding at all would only let her think she could walk all over me whenever she wanted.

"You don't know?" She forced a laugh. "What's there to know? People should worry about their own messed-up lives instead of stirring up problems in everyone else's."

All right, enough. I sat forward in my chair, an insincere smile plastered across my face. "Really? Is that what you're doing here?"

She stiffened.

Oops. Too direct.

She leaned toward me, her finger jabbing in my direction. "Now, you listen here. My mama didn't raise no fools. You divorced women think you can come here and play musical chair husbands. Maybe somebody else will end up without one instead of you. But I'll tell you what, it ain't going to be—"

"Margene." Bristol's voice, his tone sharp, sounded at the door.

We both looked up. Margene's face slid back to passive domesticity. "Tire's okay, then, Jake?"

"It's fine, Genie. Go on home and let us finish up here."

She smiled at him again and then waved her fingers at me, like we'd just been chitchatting over tea.

"I'm sorry." He closed the door and sat down behind his desk again.

"For what?" I was torn between hoping he'd witnessed her venom and praying he hadn't heard enough to make things awkward.

He grimaced, fidgeting with the pencil on his desk. "Genie has cooked up this crazy idea that you and I are looking for reasons to spend time together."

I clenched my fists in my lap. "Well, I didn't kill Doc Hallacy. Or Coach Swenson or Mrs. Parsmouth at the library." Actually, Mrs. Parsmouth had killed herself, in effect. Turned out she was one of those people who liked to suffocate herself while masturbating to heighten the pleasure, but one day the rope pulled a little too tight. Ick.

"I know that, Rennie. She's just being…" his eyes flicked up to meet mine, "paranoid."

I stood and slung my bag over my shoulder. "I have to get going."

"She doesn't mean any harm."

"Right," I muttered. I couldn't decide who I was angrier with. Surprisingly, the two top contenders appeared to be Bristol, for marrying her in the first place, and me, for getting myself into this situation. I said in a louder voice, "I'll be over at the *Gazette* for a while if you need me to sign that later." I nodded at the handwritten statement still sitting on his desk. "See you." I walked out of his office, my emotions all a jumble.

"Rennie," he called after me.

I ignored him and kept walking. *What were you expecting, Rennie?* I scolded myself in the parking lot. *Margene is a viper all right, but one he's tied to until death do they part.*

I made it all the way to my car before I realized I'd forgotten to mention Jenny Sturgeon's odd behavior to Bristol. I sighed. Maybe I'd just call later and leave a message. I didn't trust myself right now to keep from saying something I shouldn't. Of course, holding back potentially helpful information even for just a few hours might hurt the investigation...

With another sigh, I started to pivot back around toward the office, but stopped at the sight of something white on my windshield, paper of some kind trapped beneath my wipers. A sales flyer maybe. No. None of the other cars in the lot had one. Curiosity forced me forward. I pulled the paper out carefully. It looked like one of those cheap fast food napkins torn in half. On the flip side, the words 'BACK OFF' were written in what looked like Crayon or lip liner.

Mouth tight, I crumpled the napkin into my fist. Margene, of course. I opened my car and chucked the paper ball into the back seat. I didn't want to leave it lying around where someone might see it and begin asking questions. It had been pretty gutsy of her to put the note there in the first place, risking that someone might see her. Of course, the act itself was nothing illegal, and no one would likely guess the content was anything other than innocent.

I got in and slammed the door shut. "Okay, Margene. I got the message the first time," I muttered. I hadn't even done anything wrong. Although the hollow-guilty feeling inside me seemed to indicate that not doing something for lack of opportunity, and a twinge of conscience, was not quite the same thing as not doing anything at all.

SEVEN

It took me another three hours to make Bristol's changes to my articles and to turn my interview with Mrs. Mayor into something resembling a story. At a little after eight-thirty, I emailed everything to Max and slid a hard copy under his closed door. From the sounds of it, he was in a loud personal discussion with the other half of the weekend 'we.' I was half-tempted to eavesdrop to find out who was on the other end of that phone line, but my curiosity had already gotten me in enough trouble today. Plus, if I hung around too long, I'd have to listen to Max bitching about Bristol's revisions. Not worth it.

Instead, I headed home, a familiar weight settling over me. This could either be the best or worst part of my day, depending. Sometimes I loved the idea of having the night to myself, no one to answer to, no one to cook for. Well, really, no one to order out for. Still. The freedom to eat popcorn in bed without someone complaining about the crumbs or the remote control getting greasy was heady at times. Other nights, it sucked, the emptiness of my apartment only reminding me of how far I'd fallen in the last year.

When I got home, I checked on my mother first. I unlocked her door as quietly as possible and slipped in to find her already asleep in front of the television, QVC blaring. It was only quarter to nine, so by tomorrow morning, provided she slept through the night, her narcolepsy, otherwise known as anxiety and not enough sleep, should be clearing up.

I backed out as silently as I'd come in and locked her door again. I jogged up the stairs to my apartment and opened the door to Fritzy's enthusiastic greeting. She knew it was potty-time. I hooked the leash on her collar. Before taking her out, I paused at the kitchen counter to play back my answering machine. Two new messages.

The first was from Father Dan, as he preferred to be called. Father Dan was the new pastor over at First Episcopal Church of Morrisville. It also happened to be the only Episcopal church in town, so the "First" part was really just wishful thinking on the part of the founding members. Father Dan had left me a very long-winded message that amounted to him asking me to do their monthly newsletter, layout, and writing, for a quarter of what I would normally charge. Apparently, Jeanne, the church secretary, could no longer keep up with three weekly bulletins and a monthly newsletter. I couldn't blame her, especially if she was getting paid what he'd offered me.

I sighed and jotted down the information. I'd do it. I could never turn away a church, not with my conscience and my mother to hear about it. We'd gone to St. Peter's Lutheran Church as a family every Sunday until I left for college. Then my parents went together until my dad died. Now, even though my mother hadn't set foot in church for years—the common cup at communion and the sharing of the peace handshake freaked her out because of the germ-spreading potential—she was still devout.

The second message started while I was still scrawling the last of Father Dan's epic.

"Hello, Rennie," a familiar male voice said.

My heart nearly stopped in my chest because for a second I couldn't place the voice, couldn't figure out who was calling me…except maybe Bristol.

"It's been awhile, and I…I've missed talking to you." The voice deepened on the last few words. My soaring heart took a nosedive. It was Jeffrey Michael, my ex. I couldn't believe I'd forgotten the sound of his voice already, though that wasn't a bad thing as far as I was concerned. I did recognize the odd drop in timbre of his voice when he was trying to be sincere. Trying was the operative word.

"I'd hoped we could talk tonight. But…I guess you're out living it up."

Oh yeah, Jeff, the life of a single woman in Morrisville. I could peel the Ralph Lauren paint off your walls with the stories I've got.

"I'll call again. You know…just to talk. Bye, Rennie." Then a rustling sound emerged from the speaker followed by some indistinct voices and a loud click.

Six years I'd lived with that man, four married and two before that. I could count the number of times he'd initiated a conversation without a specific purpose on half a hand. My suspicion aroused by his sudden desire to chat, I hit the repeat button and leaned my head closer to the speaker at the end of his message.

Sure enough, those faint sounds were voices, but they were distinct enough if you knew what to listen for and boy, I did.

A woman's voice in a muffled whisper. "You didn't tell her."

"I know what I'm doing. You have to handle her just right or—"

The rest was lost in the click. Blood rushed through my body at a steaming mad pace, pounding in my ears. "Handled? I have to be handled? Son of a bitch."

Fritzy whined, pulling my attention back to what was important.

I rubbed the top of her head. "Sorry, baby. It's not you." She pulled at the leash, and I let her lead me out the door and down the stairs.

You didn't tell her, she'd said. She. It had to be Maria, his new wife, who also happened to be his former legal assistant/mistress. Unless he'd picked up a girlfriend again, not an impossible thing. They say the wife is the last to know, and I can vouch that's true, but it's not because you miss the signs. You see them, but just choose to give them entirely different meaning. I'd become an expert at this.

If Jeff said he was working late at the office, but he didn't answer his desk phone or cell, I didn't worry. The client had taken him out to dinner. When he started leaving credit card receipts in his pants pockets—I wasn't snooping, I was the one responsible for preparing all the dry cleaning in our house—for expensive meals at the Ritz-Carlton (two entrees, one dessert and a bottle of wine), it was just a fussy female recruit to the firm who needed to feel wooed. If calls to our house ended in hang-ups when I answered, I attributed it to a telemarketer who'd decided no one was home, even though I sometimes grabbed it on the first ring.

Keep in mind, I never asked him. I didn't want to know until the end when he started using a condom again…with me. His wife. Like his mistress was afraid of what, or who, I might have been doing in my free time. Just thinking about it made me clench my fists. Fritzy's leather leash bit into my palm.

"Son of a bitch," I muttered again. Fritzy looked around at me curiously, paused on the sidewalk in front of my mom's house.

"Sorry," I said to her again, and she returned to her investigation of an ant hill.

It had to be about the alimony, I decided. Now that he'd gotten what he wanted, he thought the price was too steep. Maybe so. I took pleasure in imagining the chunk it took out of his paycheck, but he could afford it. Of course, Jeff could always afford the expensive stuff for himself. Well, now he could afford it for me too. His phone call tonight, just to talk, was probably to try to talk me into letting him skip a payment or twelve. I'd have to decide what to do about that, but not tonight. I'd missed his call and no way was I returning it. I didn't owe him anything. The man had remarried three days after our divorce was final. On a Thursday. Who gets married on a Thursday?

I watched Fritzy sniff every blade of grass within the circumference of her leash for the perfect potty place. "If only people put in as much effort to make sure they had the right spouse, the world would be a better place," I told her. She looked up at me, her ears perked, obviously having heard a word in there that sounded like treat.

"Come on, let's go home." Exhaustion suddenly pulling at me, I tugged at Fritzy's leash. She came along amiably, stopping to do her business, which I scooped into one of those pine-scented poop bags.

A pebble or two clattered somewhere ahead of us, and Fritzy and I both looked up to see a couple out for a late night walk. I lifted my hand in greeting, but either they didn't see me or didn't care, because they crossed the street to go around us and then crossed back again.

I sighed. Greyhounds were big dogs but big babies mostly. It never failed to surprise me how many people couldn't tell the difference. To be fair, Fritzy was the only greyhound in town, maybe even in the whole county, and Morrisville didn't always react well to people, things, or events that could be considered 'outside the norm.' I knew this from personal experience.

I dropped Fritzy's bag into the trash can at the corner of the garage and led her up the stairs. After washing up, I pulled on my pajamas and searched my fridge for dinner. Another difference between me and Margene. I wouldn't know how to make a meatloaf unless the recipe came up and bit me on the butt.

I ended up eating cereal over the sink. So, this was my life now. Eating alone. Sleeping alone. Thanks to Maria and the son of a bitch. Not that I'd want him back now. I washed out the bowl and left it in the sink. I yanked the cushions off the couch, unfolded the bed, and then stared down at all the empty space. They didn't make fold out beds in a single size. Every night I crawled in feeling that much emptier. I'd tried sleeping in the middle. It didn't amount to much sleep at all.

After tossing my pillows on top of the bed, I turned off the lights and climbed in, feeling heaviness pull at my heart. This was it, my foreseeable future. I slid under the sheets and tugged the afghan off the back of the couch to curl beneath it.

I wasn't always like this. Sometimes it made me feel better to remember that, and sometimes it didn't. Once Margene Bristol would have had no reason to fear my presence, not that she had any real reason now. But things didn't go exactly as I'd expected them to, and in the process, I seemed to have lost myself and my way.

The deep dark secret that I could never tell anyone, particularly my mother, was that sometimes I missed Jeff. Not him, per se, but the comfort of someone else who knew me. The ease of talking with someone without worrying about food caught between my teeth or spitting accidentally. History. I missed having history with someone. The only problem was, you can't get history instantly. You always have to start at the beginning. That idea just exhausted me. How could I start over after exercising such poor judgment the first time? Crushing on the married sheriff probably didn't bode well for the attempt, either. Besides, I couldn't contemplate moving out of the garage apartment. How could I think about starting a new life?

Tears of frustration welling, I rolled onto my side. It wasn't fair. I hadn't asked for any of this. A year and a half ago, I'd had a very clear vision of the rest of my life. I had a job that I liked all right, a harried and hurried husband I'd certainly liked better in the earlier days of our relationship but he was nothing to complain about, yet, and the expectation of fifty or sixty years in this medium, lukewarm existence with occasional spikes of high joy at the birth of my children or chasms of deep fear at the first health scare. Not that I could have or would have articulated any of this, had someone asked.

Instead of a tepid bathwater life, I'd gotten tossed into the deep end, which boiled at times and skinned over with ice at others.

I drew my knees up to my chest, imagining as I always did that I could feel the tightness of the scar on my abdomen pulling my skin. It hadn't done that in more than a year, when it was new.

Oh, yes, there were other obstacles to starting over, in addition to my lack of good judgment regarding men. I had more baggage than O'Hare on the day after Thanksgiving. Starting with someone new would mean opening all that up again and I didn't know if I could. The date books don't give you a guide for bringing up bad, potentially relationship destroying news. Should it be your third date or maybe your fifth when you casually mention, "Oh by the way, I hope you aren't in love with the idea of biological children, because I won't be able to give them to you"? Should you wait until things seem serious? After all, nothing scares off a man like a premature discussion of children. Or, is it better to lay the 'ectopic pregnancy' and 'emergency surgery for a burst fallopian tube' cards on the table right from the beginning?

Jeff certainly hadn't been able to handle it. Oh, we'd been

falling apart long before that, but the baby had pushed us back together again. He'd started coming home on time again, and asked about names and crib sheet patterns. Then when we'd lost the baby—I'd named him Charlie after my dad even though Jeff thought this was crazy because 'it was a fetus, a clump of cells,' not a baby—we'd had nothing to hold us together.

I rolled over onto my back and stared up at the ceiling again, watching now familiar shadows dance across the darkened plain. I'd come back here to feel safe, accepted again, but the town had changed and so had I. For about the thousandth time, I found myself wondering if I'd made a mistake coming back here, running home instead of running away. Maybe it would have been easier to start again where no one knew me.

Then I remembered what Bristol had said about my mother this morning. She was better now that I was here. Clearly, even if no one else recognized it, I was doing some good by being in Morrisville.

With that comforting me, I blotted my face on my pillow case and let sleep take me in.

EIGHT

The next morning dawned bright and warm. I woke with a stuffy nose and a throbbing head, a self-pity hangover from the night before. A hot shower and a cup of my mother's coffee—I was all out at my place—cured most of that.

"You're up early for a Saturday." My mom greeted me at her back door.

I headed directly for the full coffee pot. "I could say the same to you. I saw your lights on. Hope you don't mind." I lifted a mug in her general direction.

She squinted at me. "You look terrible."

I took a deep swallow of coffee, wincing when it burned the back of my throat a little. It was still worth it. "Thanks, Mom. I just didn't get a lot of sleep." I waited for her to ask why, though I might as well have waited for her tap dance across the kitchen floor.

After an awkward pause, she asked, "Well, what are you doing up so early then? Go back to bed, get some rest."

I sipped more coffee, then shook my head. "Can't. I'm covering the Garden Show this morning, and I wanted to stop by the *Gazette* first. Find out what Max knows about a Marty Halpern."

"Marty Halpern." She frowned. "What do you want with him?"

"Gloria Lottich said he and Doc Hallacy used to be friends until they had a falling out over something to do with Maybelle." I shrugged. "Now Doc Hallacy's dead, so I thought I'd just check it out."

My mother pursed her lips. I knew she was about to impart information, gossip in her mind. Definitely one of the deadly sins. "Gloria Lottich should keep her mouth shut."

"You know something about it?" I tried to sound casual.

"Rennie," she said, "you are as see-through as a screen door in summer."

I made a come-on gesture.

She gave me a quelling look, which worked no better now than it had when I was a child. "Maybelle Hallacy died in a car accident. Marty Halpern was driving. No one knows exactly why the two of them were together or where they were going. But…they were on the road heading from Marty's place down by the lake."

"Oooh, a dangerous liaison."

"Don't you make fun, Rennie. The car slid off the road and Maybelle died by drowning, just like that Grace Kelly from the movies."

I frowned. "I think you're thinking of a Kennedy and the woman in his car."

She scowled. "Either way, it's nothing funny. Doc Hallacy was never the same after that."

"Sounds like motive to me." I swallowed the last of my coffee and set the mug in the sink.

My mother sighed, and I paused, waiting for another little gem of information. "Marty Halpern didn't kill Doc Hallacy."

"How do you know that?"

"The man's in a wheelchair. Has been since the accident." She gave me one last frown, then bustled past me to her sewing room.

Just like that, at five minutes after eight in the morning, maybe 24 hours after the murder, I was out of suspects.

I stopped by the *Gazette* to confirm what my mother had told me, though she was rarely wrong on town gossip. As much as she didn't like to spread it, she usually got it right.

When I got to the office, everything was quiet and still, and the only light was the sun coming through the windows.

"Max?" I frowned. Normally, he was the first one in, no matter how early anyone else arrived.

"Max?" I called again, a little louder. I heard a sudden rustling in the back, coming from Max's office. My heart leapt into my throat. After all, somewhere in Morrisville, a murderer roamed freely. Maybe right here at the *Gazette*. It was just up the street from the pharmacy.

I stepped toward the sound, grabbing a stapler off a desk on my way. It wasn't like I planned to staple someone to death, but I could probably bean them pretty good. The stapler was one of those old, heavy black metal ones. I paused at the edge of Max's partially opened door, preparing to shove it open, when it suddenly opened it my face.

I nearly screamed.

"Rennie, what are you doing here?" Max, dressed in rumpled clothes, frowned at me. A blanket lay in a tangled mess on the couch behind him. His chin was gray with stubble, his eyes seemed red and swollen and his hair, what was left of it in the back, stood up in a duck's tail.

I took a couple of deep breaths, then tried to swallow my heart back into place. "Looking for you." I gave a shaky laugh. "So is this how you're always here so early?" I gestured to the couch.

He seemed to realize he might not be fully put together. He made a half-hearted attempt to tuck in his shirt, but he was still frowning. "You're supposed to be covering the Garden Show."

I nodded. "I wanted to stop by here first and ask what you know about Marty Halpern."

His frown deepened, furrowing his brow. I recognized this look. It was the expression of a man digging through his mental files. Max was a Morrisville transplant, true, but he knew it and its residents better than they did. "Martin Halpern. WWII vet, married to Esther Halpern, née Johansson, for forty-nine years until her death eight years ago. He made his money owning a CAT dealership outside of Litchfield. He was injured in a car accident five years ago, left a paraplegic." Max's face relaxed a bit, smoothed out, once he finished reciting his facts. Max lived for the facts.

"What about passengers in that accident?" I persisted. "I heard Maybelle Hallacy was in the car."

"Listen, I don't want you spending too much time on this Hallacy thing," Max turned abruptly and headed deeper into his office.

I followed, gaping at him. "Are you kidding? You love these kinds of stories. You always say these are the stories that sell papers. Murder, death, mayhem, destruction." I waved my hands around in a sloppy imitation of him.

"Just drop it, Rennie." Max moved behind his desk and began rearranging stacks of paper.

"What, the Halpern angle? I mean, I agree, he's not the most likely candidate for murder, but the guy might have a motive. And—"

"The whole thing. The whole story, just forget it."

I stared at him. "What?"

"Truebeth Parkmueller died this morning. People are going to be leaving bits and pieces for her tribute article, and her family has requested that someone come by the house for pictures and quotes from them. Work on that instead." He still wouldn't look at me.

I stalked to the front of his desk and leaned forward, nearly nose to nose with him. Or I would have been, if he'd bothered to meet my eyes. "You're dropping a murder story for a tribute article? Are you smoking something? I mean, unless Truebeth Parkmueller was abducted by aliens and died while trying to escape and her body was left here with her hands still clutching evidence of her ordeal, then I don't see why you can't run with both stories."

"I didn't say I was dropping the Hallacy story. I'm giving it to Arnie." Max's tone was icy.

"Arnie? You're giving this to Arnie?" I raked my hands through my hair. "His idea of investigative journalism is finding out the daily specials at Ruby's." Arnie Ledbetter was one of the *Gazette*'s staff reporters, though not full-time; the *Gazette* could barely afford to keep Max in red pens and ugly ties. Arnie covered the town council meetings, announcements from the mayor's office, essentially the political beat, what there was of it, for Morrisville. Half the time, this meant taking whatever he got from a source and using it word for word. Once, I swear, instead of an article about topics discussed at the town council meeting, he just gave the editor, Sam Swanson at the time, the minutes. And Sam printed them. I've seen the back issue. I looked it up once, to see if that particular urban legend, so to speak, was true. Tuesday, May 19, 1992, if you don't believe me.

Max didn't respond, just sat down behind his desk, his chair wheels squeaking as he rolled himself into place.

A thought occurred to me, and I folded my arms across my middle. "If it's my writing, Max, tell me what I can do." I struggled to keep my voice even. "I know my headlines are still crap but—"

Max waved his hand dismissively. "Oh, get over yourself. This has nothing to do with you. It's just a rearrangement of talent based on demand."

I raised my eyebrows at him.

He sighed. "Everyone likes the tribute stories when you do them, Rennie, better than anyone else's."

Slightly mollified, I backed off a little. "Max, I can do both. I mean, I'll have the Parkmueller tribute done by tomorrow. And the Hallacy article isn't even close to finished, I've barely gotten started on my list of possible—"

"Enough." Max slapped his palm down flat on his desk. The sound was muffled by all the paper, but the effect was the same. I jumped.

"Drop Hallacy. Work on the Parkmueller tribute and the Garden Show, which you're going to be late for, by the way." Max lowered his eyes to the papers in front him and picked up his red pen, like I'd already left the room.

"Max…" I tried one last time.

He didn't even look up. "Rennie, if you want to keep working for the *Gazette*, you work on what I give you."

I stiffened a little at his threat. The *Gazette* was my biggest client. I needed the assignments from Max unless I wanted to start using the alimony, and based on the message I'd gotten last night, I might not have that for much longer if Maria had anything to do with it. "All right," I said quietly. "I'll see you later, Max."

He grunted in response. I closed the door to his office, gathered up the Parkmueller tribute contributions, and headed out the *Gazette*'s front door. I blinked rapidly to combat the bright sunlight and the remains of shock over what had just happened. Max had pulled me from the story. I didn't even know where to go with that or what to do with myself. I'd sort of hung my hat on the idea of filling the next few days or weeks with tracking down leads and angles for the story.

"So now what?" I muttered. I got back into my car to head to the first house in the Garden Show. I was going to be late; Max was right about that but wrong about everything else. Something seemed off with him, that was for sure. Heaven only knew what, and I didn't have time to think about it now.

* * *

I bent a few speed limits to get to the Bruebacher house, hoping everyone, including Bristol's team, would be too wrapped up in the Garden Show excitement to notice. Not that there was that much to be excited about, at least in my opinion. The 75th Annual Ladies of Morrisville Garden Show would probably work like all the ones that had come before it; I'd attended more than my share. All the participating houses, or gardens in this case, would be open for viewing at eight-thirty. The judges and interested townspeople would be allowed half an hour at each house, starting in any order. The winners would be announced at the grandstand in front of the courthouse promptly at three P.M., at which point, much oohing and aahing, mixed with a healthy dose of snippy commentary, would commence.

I pulled off to the side of the road, just down from the Bruebacher house, spraying a little bit of gravel. Enough to earn me a frown from Sheffey who was managing the crowd, keeping them moving and out of the road. I gave him a sheepish shrug and a wave, and hustled to the back of the house where everyone had gathered.

Really, Garden Show coverage was pretty easy. I'd worked this story last year for Max. Get the contestant to identify the flowers for me by color. I don't know a jonquil from a hole in the ground. Jot down a brief description, scavenge a few quotes from people who seem to know what they're talking about, and if possible, note the judges' expressions when examining the display. For whatever reason, people loved to speculate about how the decisions were made, whether or not there was some great scheme at work. If District Attorney Steve Foreman was reported to have frowned while examining what turned out to be the winning garden, then clearly some coercion had been in play to get the required unanimous vote. Tomorrow the gossips would be all atwitter with everything from bribery to sabotage as explanation.

In Morrisville, people created their own entertainment, and it was surprising how quickly you could get sucked in. I chose conspiracy as my theory. Gloria Lottich, Mrs. Mayor and Garden Club President, had won the last five years running.

Today, no one seemed particularly interested in sharing their thoughts on the dark side of the Garden Show or even speculating about the winner, at least not with me. I hadn't had time to read the *Gazette* this morning. Based on the looks I got while meandering through the crowd, my article on discovering Doc's body must have run. So, the few people who hadn't heard about what happened yesterday knew now. People whispered, tried to point semi-discreetly, but no one actually approached me to ask about it. By the third house, I began to wonder if the rumor had been twisted to make it that instead of me finding dead bodies, people dropped dead around me.

By mid-afternoon, when I headed back to the courthouse for the awards ceremony, my nose itched from all the flowers and my skin felt a little thin from all the snubbing. Nine gardens on display for competition, probably a hundred people stopping to browse at each one, and nobody, other than the contestants, had said anything more than was absolutely necessary to me. Of course, I'd skipped the Bristol house, hoping to rely on Johnny Mac's photos for that little segment of the article. Though I felt sure Margene would have had more than a few words for me.

I stood toward the back of the crowd gathering in the town square to get a better look at the proceedings. Just as Mr. Mayor, Brian Lottich, headed up the grandstand stairs to present the awards—amazing that no one had cried foul yet when his wife took first place every year—I saw Bristol coming my way.

My heart tripped. He looked good, dressed in khakis and a blue dress shirt, instead of his uniform. Just because it appeared he was headed this direction didn't mean he was looking for me, I reminded myself. After yesterday, it would probably be better if he wasn't. Either way, I would remain cool and aloof.

Bristol slowed as he got closer. "Afternoon, Rennie." He turned to face the stage so we stood side by side.

"Afternoon," I replied without taking my eyes off the stage. I longed for a cup of coffee so I'd have something to do with my hands.

"Doc Hallacy's will is being read tomorrow at one o'clock."

I looked at him in surprise. So much for cool and aloof. "Before the funeral?"

Bristol shrugged. "No law against it. The funeral won't be for another couple of days, and Hallacy requested that the will be read as soon as possible after his death."

Well, that sort of matched with what Ginjer Buchanan had said about her great-uncle wanting to return the money to whoever gave it to him. He'd wanted to do the right thing and right away, apparently.

"I want you to come, in an official capacity, of course," he said. He hesitated. "If you can."

Stunned, I turned to face him. "Are you serious?"

He nodded. "You're the closest thing I've got to a witness,

Rennie. Maybe if the murderer sees you there, it might shake something loose from him…or her. Plus, you'll get a hell of a story out of it."

Except Max had pulled me from that particular story. Crushed, I started to offer up this information to Bristol, then stopped. Arnie Ledbetter couldn't find a Klan demonstration with a police radio and his very own bed sheet. Another true story: Arnie's first attempt at undercover investigation had ended with him driving in circles, lost—*Gazette*, July 15, 1978. If I got this story and wrote it, Max would have no choice but to take it. No way he'd be able to pass up an eyewitness account of Bristol arresting a murder suspect. So, problem solved.

"You all right, Rennie?"

I grinned. "I'm great."

His mouth quirked up in a rare smile, which clutched at my heart. Jake Bristol was almost always serious, part of who he was compounded by the job. That was all right, though. He was the exact opposite of Jeffrey Michael, who was always quick to find the funny, quick to make everything a joke. My mother'd warned me against him, said any man with two first names instead of a decent surname was bound to be slick, and she was right. Jeffrey Michael had turned out to be slipperier than wet Jell-O.

"Meet me at Raines and Machesney about a quarter till. You should know, though, it's probably going to get ugly."

"You think the mysterious beneficiary will show up?" I asked.

He shrugged. "Don't know. But what I do know is Ginjer Buchanan's husband has twenty thousand dollars in gambling debt."

Ideas whirled around in my head, refusing to fall into any logical order. "The money Doc left for the Buchanan boy has to be in a trust. At least," I paused, remembering her blatant greed with a grimace, "if he knew his great-niece at all."

"I got ten bucks that says Mrs. Buchanan doesn't know that." Bristol arched his eyebrows at me.

"So that whole mad act was just because she didn't get all the money?" I grimaced. "Talk about a sense of justification."

Laura Radnor stumbled by, her children tripping her up as she tried to maneuver a stroller through the rapidly growing crowd. She still managed a decent glare at me. Feeling a bit devilish, I gave her a big smile and waved.

"I have to go," Bristol said. He nodded toward the front of the grandstand. "Genie's waiting."

I looked toward where he'd indicated to find Margene, her flowered Sunday dress a little too tight across her hips, waiting with the other contestants, her eyes focused on us.

"All right, I'll see you tomorrow. Thanks for the invite," I said, unable to wipe the grin completely from my face.

He nodded, a little tip of his head, like he was still wearing his hat, then he headed toward Margene. Chelsea, their daughter, stood nearby chatting and giggling with a group of girls. She had her mother's looks but her father's brains, at least from everything I'd heard of her. I would have loved to know her better, but that crossed lines even I avoided.

I was surprised, moments later, when Chelsea split off from her friends, with some little parting comment that left them laughing, and came in my direction, away from her parents.

She stopped a few feet away from me. She wore a tight black t-shirt with the words 'Hot Stuff' written across the front in loopy pink cursive and sparkles and skinny flare jeans. She looked almost exactly like her mother, who'd been just a little older when I'd met her for the first time, but the intelligence and suspicion in those clear green eyes belonged to her father.

"You're Rennie, right?" she asked finally.

I probably should have corrected her to say Ms. Harlow or whatever, but I'd never remember to answer to that. Instead, I nodded, not sure where this was going nor whether I wanted to follow. I looked around Chelsea to see her parents standing together near the grandstand, talking quietly. Though from their stances—his hands on his hips, head shaking, and her arms crossed and mouth pouting—it was clear that theirs was not a little love chat.

"You know my dad." Chelsea tossed the words out as a challenge.

I chose my words carefully. "I know both your parents. We were all in school together a long time ago."

"My dad says you work together, but you're not a cop."

I shook my head. "I'm a writer, a reporter for the *Gazette*. Sometimes your dad gives me information after he's caught the bad guys, and sometimes my research for stories gives him information he didn't have before." *An oversimplification to be sure, but close enough for this particular conversation*, I thought.

She rolled her eyes at me. "Whatever. I'm not five. I know how it works."

Yeah, she'd been five a whole five years ago. That was, like, practically a lifetime ago. "Okay," I said cautiously. "So what—"

"I want you to stay away from my dad." She dropped her arms to her side, her hands clutched in fists.

I stared at her, feeling as though she'd just smacked me a good one with a mallet.

Her lower lip began to tremble. "They fight all the time now. Way more than they ever used to."

I struggled to find my voice. "Chelsea, I don't know what your mother told you, but—"

She rolled her eyes again, only now they were shiny with tears. "She didn't say anything. She doesn't have to. I hear it all at night when they think I'm sleeping."

Oh, dear Lord. "Chelsea…" I reached out to touch her shoulder, but she backed away, her face crumpling.

"Just stay away, all right? Leave us alone." She pushed past me, heading away from her parents and the crowd. I watched her go, torn between following her to make sure she was all right and wanting to hide in the nearest hole in the ground. Those people standing close enough to have heard what Chelsea said were now carefully avoiding looking in my direction. My face felt like it was on fire.

I had to get out of there. Within an hour, the whole town would know what had just happened. I made myself wait, though, until Mr. Mayor announced the winners. Fleeing now would only give everyone more to talk about and probably confirm their suspicions.

Mrs. Mayor, Gloria Lottich, won the first prize, as usual. In an equally unsurprising turn, Margene Bristol took second. Comforting, I guess, that even as my little world collapsed in on me, some things never changed.

NINE

Good God. As I drove home, Chelsea Bristol's words, and the way she broke into tears, kept playing over and over in my head, like a video loop from hell. I wanted to be unconscious. Or out of town. Or out of town *and* unconscious. How much of a horrible person do you have to be to make a ten-year-old cry? The thought crossed my mind that perhaps Margene had put her up to it, after our little tiff the other day. No...Chelsea's emotions were too genuine, too heart-wrenching.

Well, that just settled it. I'd have to stay away from Bristol, even in an official capacity.

How do you plan to do that, a sneaky voice inside my head asked. He's your best source for the *Gazette*.

I'd just have to refuse all the articles that might require the sheriff as a source...and kiss good-bye any hope of earning enough money to live on, let alone getting full-time employment from Max. Not that he'd be all that displeased to let me go, or so it seemed lately. I wasn't having a very good day. Of course, little did I know, it was about to get worse.

I had a few minutes before I was due at the Parkmueller house, so I stopped by home to take Fritzy out and regain some of my composure. I couldn't show up at the Parkmueller house all teary-eyed and out of sorts. People tended not to talk to you like that. Instead, they'd persist in asking you what was wrong, and whatever story might actually be there would be lost under your own.

After I walked Fritzy, I checked my messages. Four hang-ups. *Jeffrey Michael trying to handle me*, I thought. I really didn't need him today. I had one real message from Johnny Mac, saying he'd meet me over at the Parkmueller house after the Garden Show.

I'd left my apartment and was backing my car into the alleyway next to my mother's house before I noticed something odd. The garage door was up, and my mom's car was gone.

Frowning, I put the car in park, risking a honk from an angry neighbor for blocking the alleyway.

For whatever reason, the planners who had designed this neighborhood had inserted two alleyways. The one off of Oak ran behind all the houses on our block. The other, off of Fairlane, connected with the one off Oak. My mother's house sat at the intersection of the two alleys. Right now, my car blocked both of them.

I jogged up to her house and knocked on the door. When there was no response, I tried the handle and found it unlocked—a bad small town habit I'd fallen into again myself. The house was dark and still.

Well, it wasn't impossible that she could have gone out, I thought, closing the door. I turned toward the deck stairs. She used to be all over town before she got sick, or thought she got sick. Now, she was afraid to drive to the grocery store alone, for fear a heart attack, stroke, aneurysm or a fit of narcolepsy might strike.

It was much more likely she'd gotten the nerve to go somewhere alone than someone had stolen her car from a closed up garage in broad daylight.

Back in my car, I dug out my cell phone and tried her cell phone, a Christmas present from me last year. It went straight to voice mail. It could mean she was talking to someone, but it was more likely she'd forgotten to turn it on.

I closed the phone and dropped it back into my bag, fighting the urge to panic. *Okay, Rennie, deep breath, I coached myself. She's an adult, your mother, for crying out loud. If she wants to take a drive, she doesn't need your permission. She can handle it on her own. It's a good thing she feels strong enough to be out and about.*

After repeating that to myself a few times, I was able to put the car in drive and head over to the Parkmuellers. Caring for a sick parent, sick mentally or physically, changes you. The security you once knew, even as a grown child of that person, disappears under the effects of the role-reversal. Frankly, I was still adjusting.

I didn't see Johnny Mac's beat up Ford Escort anywhere near the Parkmueller house, so I parked on the street, lowered the window, and waited. I could have gone in without him, but I wanted to find out if he had any more information on what Max thought we were supposed to accomplish here. Interviewing the deceased's relatives for the tribute article was a little strange. We got a quote from them, here and there, usually prepared ahead of time. Nothing big enough to warrant pulling me off the Hallacy story.

Unless, of course, it was me or my writing that had motivated Max's sudden change of mind. I dropped my head back against the headrest. Great. I learn I'm a horrible writer and a sucky human being all in the same day. I flashed back to Chelsea's tear-stained face.

Sucky? See, there you go. No wonder Max won't hire you, you go making up words and—

A sharp rap sounded on the passenger side window.

I jumped and looked over to find Johnny Mac's grinning face.

I lowered that window. "You scared me to death."

"Well, I've been calling your name and waving to you for about a half a block." He pointed ahead of me where I could see his battered and rusty car now parked. "Whoever he is, he's not worth it, if you have to think that hard about it." His grin grew wider.

Normally, I loved Johnny Mac. Max had sort of inherited him from Sam, the previous editor. Johnny Macintyre was a senior at Morrisville High. He'd started hanging out at the *Gazette* when he turned thirteen, offering to take pictures for free. He planned to be a world-famous photographer and wanted to get started on his dream right away. Sam had always turned him down, preferring to take the pictures himself. Personally, I think that's because Sam secretly harbored the dream he was a world-famous photographer. He wasn't. Max was no fool, though. Johnny had talent. Free talent was even better. Johnny was a good kid, who'd grown up, to sound like my grandmother, into a nice young man and a bit of a flirt. He was cute—dark curly hair, blue eyes and freckles—in that good guy kind way that would probably earn him more hearts than he knew what to do with once he hit college.

Today, though, his sense of humor hit a little too close to home. The heat I'd only just managed to vanquish from my face returned with a vengeance. "Shut up." I glared at him. I put the windows up, grabbed my bag and got out of the car.

"So what's the story with this place?" Undisturbed by my momentary wrath, Johnny loped beside me as I headed up the broken and uneven sidewalk to the big two-story brick house.

"I have no idea." Then I confessed, "But Max pulled me off the Hallacy story for it."

Johnny stopped dead, his eyes gone wide. "You're kidding."

It did my ego good that disbelief was his first reaction. "Nope."

"Then this could be something really awesome." He caught up with me, pulled his camera strap off his shoulder and dropped it around his neck with enthusiasm.

"Yeah, or Max is nuts," I muttered, thinking of him giving my

Hallacy story to Arnie Ledbetter.

"Have you noticed that too?" Johnny asked, startling me.

Now it was my turn to stop. "What do you mean?" I tried to sound casual.

Johnny shook his head with a laugh. "No. You can't work that on me. I've seen you in action too many times."

I pursed my lips in exasperation. "Fine. He gave Arnie my story, he seems to be sleeping at the office and he was in an argument on the phone with…someone." I didn't want to give Max's secret away. If he actually had a secret, that is. All I had was speculation. "What've you got?"

Johnny gave a low whistle. "Wow. To Ledbetter, huh?"

I nodded.

He shrugged. "I don't have anything to top that. But he sent me here to take pictures and you know how he is about photos for tribute articles."

If Max was finicky about headlines, he was fanatical about photos. No grip and grins, no animals dressed like people, and no photos for no-news articles, a classification that our tribute articles fell into. Normally, there would be one picture of Truebeth Parkmueller and that would be it. Otherwise, you'd have family trying to insert photos of the deceased from birth until age eighty-six, a favorite car, the first pet, etc. So Max was pretty much breaking his second commandment. His first? Thou shalt have no shitty headlines.

"Anything else?" I started up the porch steps to the front door.

"Max doesn't have kids, right?" Johnny asked. He was good at taking photos, not so much with paying attention to detail.

I frowned at him. "No. Why?"

He shrugged. "Cause, I've seen him at school twice now."

"The high school?" I asked, like Johnny went to school

89

someplace else.

Johnny nodded.

It didn't make sense, Max being over there. Unless he was working on some kind of story, an exposé or something.

The front door opened, letting out a gust of stale air, before I could ask Johnny any more questions or even ring the bell.

"You must be from the newspaper." A slim woman, probably in her late forties, her blonde hair escaping a blue kerchief tied on her head, stood in the doorway beckoning us in. "I'm Liz Merritt, Truebeth's granddaughter. I've been watching for you. I wasn't sure if the doorbell worked or if we'd even hear it in here." She gave a light laugh that sounded a little forced.

When she stepped back to let us in, I saw why.

"Holy Mother of—" Johnny murmured.

I elbowed him sharply in the ribs.

Piles and piles of newspapers and magazines were stacked everywhere for as far as the eye could see. On the stairs leading up, the one distinguishable architectural feature, the stacks were only about knee-height, but otherwise the paper was piled higher than my head.

Liz gave another nervous laugh. "Yes, Grandmother was quite the collector."

"No shit," Johnny muttered. My elbow didn't move quite fast enough that time.

"So, uh," I tried to think of what to say. "I guess you'll be in town for awhile then."

"Oh, no," she said with a bit of a shudder. "We're selling this place as is."

I gaped at her.

"There are hardwood floors under here." She tapped her foot against a lower pile, making it wobble ominously. "This house could be quite the bargain," she said. "Besides, there could a fortune in here somewhere."

Or an avalanche, I thought. Now, that would make one hell of a story. Reporter and photographer trapped for years inside house of paper.

"Here, come this way." Liz started down a narrow path toward the back of the house. Her thin shoulders brushed the stacks on either side. Johnny and I both had to turn sideways to follow her. "You'll probably want to see her other things, too."

"Sweet." Johnny was clearly fascinated by the weirdness factor of this one.

"Apparently, Grandmother also had a penchant for Cool Whip containers."

Oh, man. The only story here was Liz Merritt's gall at trying to sell this place off to some unsuspecting sucker. Whoever it turned out be, I'd bet they'd get a good price.

* * *

After narrowly escaping the Parkmueller house—one bedroom upstairs was entirely devoted to towering piles of old records without their covers; one misstep and someone might have lost a head or at least an eye—I went home to try to get my notes to congeal into some kind of story and to finish my write up on the Garden show. Normally, I didn't work on *Gazette* stuff at home. Max was a much better motivator than my books, my television, Fritzy, everything that called for me to avoid writing, but I didn't feel like facing him again today. Actually, I didn't feel like facing anyone in what remained of today.

Except my mother, that is.

I shoved my laptop off my legs and stood up from the couch to stretch and look out the window. It was almost six o'clock, and my mother hadn't returned home yet. I was tempted to call the

Sheriff's Office, except if she turned up safe and sound, she'd never forgive me. That, and breaking my vow to stay away from Bristol the same day I made it didn't seem like the best idea.

I'd give her until ten o'clock, I decided. If she wasn't back by then, I'd call down to the office and get Sheffey or Barnes to do whatever they could do. They'd probably call Bristol, but at least I wouldn't have to.

I was fixing myself another bowl of cereal for dinner—I had to get to the grocery store again, I was all out of microwave meals—when I heard the gravel crunch outside under the weight of an approaching car. I carried my dinner to the window and watched as my mother's car pulled into the space next to mine. The garage only had room for one car, so my dad, a long time ago, had spread gravel over a section of our yard between the back deck and the garage, creating another parking area, just off the alleyway to Fairlane. My mother never parked there, preferring the safety of the garage for her Camry. I, however, always parked the BMW in the open and left the doors unlocked at night, hoping someone would steal it for parts so I could call and give Jeff the bad news.

I watched as my mom got out of her car and closed the door quietly, her hand following it all the way to the frame of the car, instead of just shoving it and letting the hinges do the rest. Then, with a furtive glance up at my apartment—I stepped back from the window a little, though I was pretty sure she couldn't see me—she hurried up the deck stairs to the back door. Oddly enough, she was wearing one of her church outfits, a black suit I'd gotten her a number of years ago as a present. She seemed unharmed.

I sat back down on the couch and tucked my legs under me. I still had no idea where she'd been. Not that she owed me any explanation, but at least she could have told me something so I wouldn't worry. Unless she hadn't wanted me to know. Unless she thought I'd be upset.

I straightened up. Could she have been on a date? The idea sent a tremor of relief and sadness through me. I'd told her a couple of months ago she should get out there and start meeting people. She hadn't protested as loudly as she had when I'd first mentioned it two years ago. That would make sense for her to be dressed the way she was, but why wouldn't she tell me?

My gaze zeroed in on a picture of the three of us, Mom, Dad and me, hanging on the wall across from me. It'd been taken at my college graduation, just a few years before he died. Tears stung my eyes. I loved my dad. Even after this much time, I still missed him with an ache that felt like it would never dull. He'd been quite the pun maker, one right after the other, in a long string, challenging me to come up with the next one. When he'd retired from his managerial position at the Smithery, he'd devoted his free time to woodworking, something he'd always loved. That was my dad, the smell of fresh sawdust and a big, infectious laugh.

I dried my face with the back of my hand. Maybe that's why she hadn't told me. Despite my happiness for her trying to find someone to spend her time with, I still would have been upset.

I'd have to talk to her, get this straightened out. Just not tonight.

I resettled the laptop on my legs. I'd finally finished the Garden Show results story and emailed it to Max. He didn't like email nearly as well as hard copy; I think it was all about him getting to use his favorite red pen. I couldn't seem to get started on the Parkmueller story, though. The tribute I had well in hand. Truebeth's full name, by the way, was Gertrude Elizabeth. I would have gone by Truebeth too. It was the story on the sale of the Parkmueller house, what Max had to be after, that just wouldn't come. I had plenty of interesting details, the house was jam packed with them, and an angle: Liz Merritt's hidden treasure idea. However, my brain refused to settle down into the work of making paragraphs. Too many questions and too many emotions trying to push forward in the silence of an evening alone.

Finally, I set the laptop on the footlocker from college I used as a coffee table and pulled out a notebook and pen from my bag on the floor near the couch. Writing for me, the act of a pen to page, was therapeutic, always had been. Sometimes it had to be the freeform expression of whatever I was feeling instead of whatever I was supposed to be writing before I could get out of my own way. You can imagine this was hell on deadlines occasionally, especially in college as an English major, but it couldn't be avoided.

So, I started a list of all the things bugging me, things that wouldn't leave me alone. Doc Hallacy's murder. Max pulling me off the Hallacy story and his other bizarre, inexplicable behavior, like showing up at the high school. My inability to buckle down and finish the Parkmueller story. Jeff's message last night and the part of it I wasn't supposed to hear. My mother's unexplained absence this afternoon. Chelsea Bristol's accusations and tears at the Garden Show.

When I was done, I stared down at the list. No wonder I couldn't concentrate. I didn't even know where to start with this list. Finally, I picked my mother. She had hurt and worried me by leaving without telling me what was going on, by hiding something from me. As usual, despite my guilt, I felt a bit resentful at expending so much energy worrying simply because she refused to take care of herself. She could get help, mental help, but she didn't. Because she couldn't believe there was nothing physically wrong with her. At least not wrong to the degree she preferred to imagine. I'd have to talk to her. Tell her that if she wanted me to stay close, which she did, then she'd have to make a few concessions, like telling me she was leaving, though not necessarily where she was going, when she disappeared for half a day.

Jeff. Jeff could keep calling and hanging up to his heart's content. He'd agreed to the alimony payment and that was that. No, I didn't exactly need the money right now, which caused a squishy guilty feeling in me. In trying to go back on his word, though, he was trying to take advantage of me. He'd done that quite enough while we were married, thank you very much. I wouldn't let him off the hook for the money, and if he tried to get away with not sending it, I'd take him to court. Jeffrey Michael's worst nightmare, public embarrassment. Unless, of course, I relented slightly, he had a good reason for asking. Like six months to live.

On to Max. I'd wanted to quit when he pulled me off that story. I still could, but Max was the most likely employer for me in town, so I wasn't sure if I should. I could confront him, try to get the straight answers behind all this weird behavior, but Max could be just as good at hiding the truth as he was at ferreting it out. Besides, there was no proof that taking me off the story was related to him sleeping in his office, getting into arguments on the phone, and showing up at the high school. Except maybe as evidence of him making unusual decisions due perhaps to some other pressure in his life of which I was unaware. I'd have to keep an eye on him, try to help him when I could. He was my friend, sort of, as well as my client.

Doc Hallacy's murder. Bristol would eventually catch the guy who did it. I knew that, but he was limited by the ways and means of the law. I wasn't. At least not as much. I wasn't on the story anymore, though, and Arnie was, despite the fact his instincts, if he had any, would certainly lead him in the wrong direction. 'Course, no one said I couldn't continue to investigate Hallacy's murder as long as I didn't let Max know about it. Actually, that wasn't quite true—someone had said I couldn't continue investigating Hallacy's death, though in not so many words. Which led me to my final problem.

Chelsea Bristol. She'd looked right through me and seen exactly what I feared. I didn't know what to do…except stay away from Jake Bristol as I'd already vowed to do. I wanted to apologize to her, to tell her it didn't mean anything. My friendship with Bristol was harmless, except for Margene's complete overreaction to it. Then again, maybe that was enough. Chelsea's pain had been real and I couldn't justify my feelings over hers, even though I knew in the deepest part of my heart nothing would ever happen between Bristol and me. I'd have to leave off. If I wanted to investigate Hallacy's murder, I'd have to do so without Bristol's knowledge or help, which meant avoiding the will reading tomorrow, as much as it nearly killed me to think of doing so. I had no choice in the matter.

Calmer, if not happier, I closed the notebook and returned to my laptop for the Parkmueller house story. This time, with my notebook holding all my thoughts, worries and feelings, the words flowed freely, and the story developed. By ten, I'd emailed the story to Max and climbed into bed, feeling resolved and resigned to my new lot in life.

That lasted about ten hours, give or take.

TEN

The next morning, a knock sounded at my door before I'd even had a chance to get showered for church. Expecting my mother with a lame excuse for her disappearance yesterday, I pulled open the door without first checking to see who was there.

I was startled to see Bristol standing outside my door, his hat in his hands. He'd never been here before.

"Hi, Rennie."

I nodded. "Bristol." I wasn't sure whether to ask him in or not. The truth was, in spite of Chelsea's words yesterday and my own promises to myself, just seeing him tugged hard on something within me. His hair was still damp from the shower, and he just looked...clean and good in his perfectly ironed uniform. Margene's work, no doubt. She was the right wife for him in that respect. Maybe in all respects. "What do you want?"

"Can I come in?" He kept his eyes trained on my face.

I looked down at myself, in my faded but comfy pink cotton pajamas and no bra, and felt heat creep into my face. "Yeah." I backed away from the door to let him in and yanked the blanket off my bed to cover myself up.

Bristol stood awkwardly in the middle of the dim room, turning his hat by the brim in his hands. With the couch still folded out into a bed, there wasn't any place to sit except the lone barstool at the breakfast bar. It all looked very sad and pathetic. Welcome to my life, I wanted to say, chagrin burning through me at Bristol seeing this part of my life, but I didn't.

Fritzy stood and stretched on her cushion, her joints popping.

She stuck her nose cautiously in Bristol's direction. Without hesitation, he knelt and extended his hand for her to sniff.

"You are a pretty one, aren't you?" He stroked the top of her head gently.

For some reason, that pulled at my heart so strongly I had to swallow back tears. I cleared my throat. "Careful, she'll—"

Fritzy butted her head into his chest, begging for more attention. I knew the feeling.

"—get you full of hair. Sorry about that."

"It's all right. I haven't been around a dog since I was a kid."

No doubt Margene would never have allowed all the hair and occasional patches of dog drool that decorated my place.

He gave Fritzy one last pat on the head and then straightened up.

"Fritzy, lay down," I said. She acquiesced with a groan, expressing her discontent at being pulled away from a friendly hand.

I folded my arms across my chest. "So what are you doing here?"

"I thought you might not come this afternoon, to the will reading, after…after yesterday," he said.

So he'd gotten Chelsea to confess what had happened. He was, after all, the sheriff. That, or he'd heard the rumors that were bound to be circulating. Heat swallowed my face whole. "I'm not. Max pulled me off the story." I didn't bother to add that it had happened yesterday morning, long before I'd accepted Bristol's invitation to go.

He leaned back a little, startled. "He did? Why?"

I shrugged. "Something about a rearrangement of talent. I'm working on the Parkmueller tribute." I paused, but couldn't help myself from going on. "Max gave the Hallacy story to Arnie

Ledbetter."

"Arnie?" Bristol asked in clear disbelief. "Arnie couldn't find his own car in the parking lot."

"I know." I shrugged, feeling a bit of vindication Bristol saw things the same way I did. 'Course, that was always the way it was. One of the reasons we worked well together…or *had* worked well together. "So you should talk to Arnie about the will reading, okay?" I turned my back to him, pretending to straighten something on the breakfast bar.

I heard Bristol step closer. "Listen, Rennie, I still want you to come to the will reading."

"I don't think that's a good idea." I refused to turn around to look at him, knowing I would give in if I did.

"I meant what I said. You are the closest thing to a witness I've got, and sometimes seeing expressions on people's faces when they think we know something we don't leads us in the right direction."

I didn't say anything, just straightened a stray pencil into perfect alignment with the napkin holder next to it.

"Please, Rennie." He stood now maybe a foot from me. I could feel his closeness.

"All right." I found myself saying the words before I'd even realized my resolve had crumbled.

"Thank you," he said, relief evident in his voice. "I'll see you this afternoon, quarter to one at Raines and Machesney."

"Got it." I nodded, all the while feeling a thick layer of guilt for having agreed, and despite myself, a tiny spark of joy that my friendship, for lack of a better word, with Bristol wasn't over. At least not yet.

I heard him back away toward the door. Only then did I feel it was safe to turn around. I watched as he paused to rub Fritzy's head once more and then he left, closing the door firmly behind him.

I walked over and flopped onto my bed, still wrapped in my blanket. Going with him this afternoon would be a mistake. Not on his part, I didn't think, but mine. Bristol would never cheat on Margene. He just wouldn't. I knew he cared about me, my safety, my well-being. He may have enjoyed my company and felt the tug of attraction between us, but that's as far as it went for him. He would never do anything about it. That's why he could come to my apartment to plead with me to go to the will reading and still be a good husband and father. His wife and daughter, in his mind, were overreacting, being paranoid.

Only I knew they were right. Because they were worried about me, about what I might do, not him. Sometimes, so was I.

* * *

"You can't be here. This is a private proceeding." Machesney of Raines and Machesney, Attorneys-at-Law, was very nervous, even for a lawyer. He pulled a starched square handkerchief out of his suit coat pocket and wiped the top of his balding head. To my mind, that meant he knew something, probably something big.

"This is a murder investigation, Mr. Machesney. I'm sure you understand how this will reading could be important to us," Bristol said. His hands rested on his hips, his jacket pulling slightly reveal his holster.

Machesney's eyes darted to me, standing a little behind and to the side of Bristol. "You may stay, if no one objects," he told Bristol. "But she remains out here." Machesney pointed to a stuffy-style wing chair behind us, just outside the door to his private office. "I won't have the media turning this private matter into a three-ringed circus."

Ooh, Machesney knew something indeed. As for the event

turning into a circus, I was tempted to look behind me to see if I'd missed all the major news crews arriving.

Bristol raised his eyebrows at me, questioning.

"Yeah, it's okay." I backed away from Machesney's door and dropped into the chair. This was a lot closer than I would have dared to come without Bristol's invitation, so it worked out fine for me. Not as fine as it could have been, but oh well. At least out here, I'd see everyone, including the mysterious beneficiary, come and go, and get a look at all the reactions.

Bristol nodded and followed the sweating Mr. Machesney into his office. About five minutes later, Ginjer Buchanan, arms full of a runny-nosed Junior, and her husband strode in. Ginjer paused to frown at my presence, then hurried in, the call of money too strong for her to resist long enough to ask why I was here.

The Buchanans were followed by Jenny Sturgeon, who kept her head tucked down like she didn't see me, and Kitty Alexander, wearing what was probably a size zero black suit and riding a wave of her own perfume.

To my surprise, the door closed behind Kitty as if no one else was expected. I guess I'd thought the mysterious benefactor might be somebody I hadn't already thought of. Then again, perhaps Doc Hallacy hadn't gotten around to changing his will. Perhaps Ginjer Buchanan and her pony-loving husband would be bumped up to the top of Bristol's suspect list after all.

I slumped back in the stiff chair to wait. After about fifteen minutes, a shrill shriek rent the hushed stillness around me. Turns out, I didn't need to worry about the door between me and the action. With Ginjer's voice, it might as well have not been there at all.

"What do you mean, we can't touch the money 'til he's eighteen?"

I smiled. Bristol was ten bucks richer. I sat up, fishing in my bag for my little tape recorder. This might get me some very good quotes.

About twenty minutes later, Ginjer, husband and sobbing child flew out of the office, as though they were being chased. Kitty Alexander stormed out immediately after.

"Ms. Buchanan, do you have any comment on the proceedings?" I called after her. She didn't even pause long enough to give me a dirty look.

Kitty Alexander turned on her pencil-thin heel. "You want a comment? I'll give you one."

I extended my tape recorder toward her, taking care to keep my head turned away from the cloying scent of roses.

"How dare that old man have the nerve." Her hands were clenched in fists, putting her perfectly manicured nails in peril.

"Nerve to do what exactly?" The words sounded a bit garbled, as I was trying to breathe through my mouth without looking like it.

"He willed me parking spaces that are already mine."

When my expression apparently didn't register enough disbelief for her tastes, she threw hands into the air and stalked off toward the door.

"Rennie."

I turned to see Bristol in the doorway, a frown carving his face. "I need to go back to the office, pick up Barnes."

"What happened?" I lowered the tape recorder to my side.

"The major beneficiary to Doc's fortune, and I do mean fortune, is Marty Halpern."

Marty Halpern, the one-time friend, the one responsible for the death of Maybelle Hallacy, the one who might have been…canoodling with her before her death. "*The* Marty

Halpern?"

He nodded, seeing I understood what that meant.

"But he was permanently crippled after that accident a few years back. He's in a wheelchair now."

Bristol settled his hat on his head again. "People in wheelchairs can't kill someone?"

"Well," I paused, trying to imagine how that would play out. "The angle would be all wrong for him to have killed Doc. I'd think it be hard to work up enough force to—"

"Rennie, even people in wheelchairs can pick up the phone and hire someone to do the dirty work. Particularly a someone who stood to gain 1.2 million from it."

My mouth fell open. "Dollars?"

He nodded.

Just like that, Marty Halpern, wheelchair or not, became the prime suspect in my mind. For about a million reasons.

* * *

Marty Halpern still lived in his house by the lake. I'd have thought he would have found it hard to face that water every day, after what happened to Maybelle, particularly if his relationship with her had been what my mother had hinted. That was before I knew him.

"What the hell do you want?" he greeted us at his front door.

Bristol, Barnes, and I stood clustered on his small front stoop. Bristol had asked me to come along for the same reason he'd invited me to the will reading—bait, essentially. I'd thought about refusing, but if I didn't go with him, I'd have to go on my own later, as part of my unofficial investigation, which wouldn't be good if Halpern turned out to be the murderer. Plus, Barnes was with us. He'd said, with his typical, asinine sense of humor, that he didn't want to miss it if I managed to 'sniff out' Halpern as the murderer.

"Martin Halpern?" Bristol asked.

"Well, you came to my house, didn't you? Who'd you expect?" He rolled his chair back allowing us in. "Damn fools," he muttered under his breath.

"Mr. Halpern." A stocky woman, dressed in green scrub pants and one of those cutesy decorated smocks covered with teddy bears, came racing from the back of the house. "You know you're supposed to let me answer the door."

He glared up at her. "Shame when a man with wheels instead of legs beats you to the door."

She pursed her lips and exhaled loudly through her nose. After one last exasperated look at him, she turned to us. "I'm Mr. Halpern's nurse. Can I help you gentlemen, and lady, with something?"

She moved slightly to stand in front of her charge, who promptly bumped into her with his wheelchair. "Now don't get your panties up in a bunch, Maude. They're here about the money. Ain't you?" He stared up at us, his glasses, the largest feature on his wizened face, reflecting the hallway light and hiding his eyes.

"I assume Mr. Machesney has been in contact with you then." Though I couldn't see Bristol's face, I could hear the tightness in his voice. Sounded like he'd hoped to surprise Halpern with his sudden good fortune and catch his reaction.

"Yeah, I heard from him. You can tell him to keep the damn money. I don't want a penny of none of that." He rolled off to the right, into what looked like a parlor turned hospital room. Various machines stood clustered around a hospital bed in the center of the room. A shiny walker in the far corner was draped in clothing, much like how I'd used my treadmill in Chicago.

"I believe Mr. Halpern is finished speaking with you, and it's time for his dialysis." She tried to edge us toward the door. Bristol didn't move.

"Mr. Halpern." Bristol raised his voice to reach into the other room. "We'd like to ask you a few more questions. That okay with you?"

"Whatever will keep her from chasing after me with a needle again." He gave a rusty laugh.

Nurse Maude, whether that was her first name or last, stiffened and then backed away to let us through to the other room.

"I assure you he has the finest care available," she said in an undertone. Then she followed us into the room. "Some of the older patients tend to be a bit cantankerous—"

"Nurse...Maude, is it?" Bristol asked.

She nodded.

"We're not here to investigate you, unless someone like Mr. Halpern files a complaint."

Halpern let out another cackle. "Woohoo, got you now, Maudie."

"We're here tonight to talk to Mr. Halpern about a murder," Bristol finished. Mr. Halpern looked distinctly less joyous at this news.

"I don't know nothing about that." He stared down at his hands folded in his lap. Then he looked up. "Besides, what are you wasting your time on me for? You see how I am." He banged his fist on the armrest of the chair.

"Where were you yesterday morning between the hours of six and eight A.M.?" Bristol asked.

"I coated myself in fairy dust and flew over to the pharmacy and killed Doc Hallacy. That what you want to hear?"

Nurse Maude gasped. "Indeed, you did no such thing."

I guess the whole fairy dust part had gone right over her head, indicative of her sense of humor, or lack thereof. For a moment, I felt sorry for Halpern.

Nurse Maude straightened her teddy-bear covered smock. "Mr. Halpern cannot drive at all or leave the house without assistance. Yesterday morning, he was here, sleeping until nine."

"You live here?" Bristol asked.

Maude shifted a bit, fingering her gray curls. "I'm here every day, but I only stay the night three times a week. He usually doesn't need help after I get him into bed at night, and he has an emergency call button," she added defensively.

"Were you here Thursday night?" Bristol asked.

"No, but he couldn't have—"

"Thank you very much, ma'am," Bristol said. Then he looked to Halpern. "You want to add to or change your statement, sir?"

Halpern shifted a little in the chair, fiddling with a loose thread on his red flannel shirt. I was surprised Super Nurse Maude didn't swoop in and cut it for him. "I didn't kill him," he said finally. "If I was going to do that, I'd've done it years ago. When he killed Maybelle."

A stunned silence held in the room for a moment. Finally, I said, "Mr. Halpern, Maybelle died in a car accident. You were driving."

Halpern squinted up at me. "I know what happened, missy. I was there, weren't I?"

"Okay, but you just said—"

"I know what I said. Jesus Christ on stilts. How far did they lower them standards to let women be police?"

"Just what did you mean then?" Bristol intervened before I could do more than shoot Halpern a dirty look. No one bothered to correct his misapprehension about my profession.

Halpern sighed. "The young lady had it right. I was driving the car, hit an icy patch, and went straight into Lake Morris." He looked down at his hands again. "By the time I come to, Maybelle was under the water, had been for awhile." He paused. "She was cold and still. Her eyes were still watching me, like she'd died waiting for me to save her. But I didn't, couldn't."

"Her death was ruled an accident," I spoke up quietly.

"Yeah, an accident. I suppose it was. But wouldn't have been no accident if it weren't for Hallacy."

"What do you mean, Mr. Halpern?" Bristol asked. "Did Mr. Hallacy sabotage your car, cause the accident somehow?"

"Young man, are you paying attention?" he snapped. "I said I hit an icy patch, lost control. Straight through the guard rail." Halpern stopped talking, and just when I thought Bristol would have to prompt again, he continued.

"Maybelle wouldn't leave him. I found her first, courted her through high school, but when I left for the war, he moved in, snatched her up."

I frowned. Gloria Lottich made the break in Halpern and Hallacy's friendship sound more recent than WWII era. I kept my mouth shut, hoping he'd continue.

"I got my own wife, had kids, but I never forgot Maybelle. When my own Esther, God love her, passed on, Maybelle came to comfort me. She started visiting me again. One thing led to another. Things were no different now than they was then."

I fought to keep an even face. Doc Hallacy had been seventy-eight when he died. If Hallacy and Halpern were the same age, this hot little affair started when Halpern and Maybelle were in their early seventies. I fought hard not to come up with a mental image of that.

"Anyway, Hallacy found out and Maybelle came out to end it with me. Only she couldn't tell me here, she was too broke up about it." His voice began to crack. "She waited until we were in the car." A tear slid out from under his glasses down his withered cheek. Maude, her hand pressed to her mouth and her eyes damp, touched his shoulder. Halpern didn't protest.

"One last question, Mr. Halpern. Why did Doc leave you his money?" Bristol asked.

I knew the answer to that one. "He felt he owed you, didn't he? He would have been nothing without Maybelle, and he took her from you." That was the only way I could make sense out of Doc's comment to Ginjer that he'd given the money to the one who gave it to him, albeit indirectly.

Halpern nodded. "He left a letter for me with his lawyer and that's what it said, pretty much." He looked up at me, his eyes still wet. "But money's a cold comfort when you're old and alone. I'd have rather had Maybelle."

We all shifted a bit, with me swallowing hard against the lump in my throat. I wasn't a deputy, but I had the feeling it might not do the reputation well to cry during part of an official investigation.

"Thank you for your time, Mr. Halpern," Bristol said quietly. "We'll be in touch if we have more questions."

Halpern just grunted at us, and we showed ourselves out. Bristol and Barnes led the way back to the car with me picking up the rear.

"You get a list of inventory from the pharmacy?" Bristol asked Barnes.

"Yep."

"Did you check it to see if the murder weapon was part of his inventory or something the killer brought in?" Bristol asked as we climbed in the car.

"Hallacy carried the canes, but I don't know if that one

belonged to his stock or not." Barnes steered the car back out onto the main road.

"See if you can find out."

"You can't seriously think that man got out of his wheelchair and killed someone." I leaned forward in the back seat.

"Somebody's lying somewhere, Rennie."

"Doesn't mean it's Halpern," I pointed out.

"Ren-tin-tin doesn't get the scent here," Barnes muttered. I glared at his reflection in the rearview mirror.

Bristol ignored the exchange. "Did you see what he had in that room of his?"

I thought back. "A bed, a bunch of machines…" I trailed off, a realization sending a shiver through me. "A walker, in the corner. Just like the ones in Doc Hallacy's window."

"You don't have a walker, if a man can't walk," Barnes piped in.

"You have to wonder if he's missing a cane," Bristol said.

I sank back into the seat, kicking myself all the way back to the Sheriff's Office for not seeing what they'd seen.

When Bristol got out of the car and headed toward the office, I called after him. "You really think he did it? Halpern, I mean." I walked around the car so we wouldn't have to shout to be heard.

He lifted a shoulder. "I'm not ready to rule him out yet."

I sighed and dropped my gaze to the ground.

"Rennie." I looked up to see a smile tugging at Bristol's mouth. The very second one I'd gotten. "Cut yourself some slack. This is my job, not yours." He reached out like he was going to pat me on the arm, but he caught himself and pulled back.

My heart stuttered. After a second, I realized we were both just standing there in silence, looking at each other.

"Sorry." He pulled his gaze from mine.

I swallowed hard, trying to find my voice. "For what?" This was the perfect opportunity to say something, but I didn't know if there was anything that could be said.

Bristol took a deep breath. "I—"

"Sheriff!" Sheffey came running out of the office, his tie flapping up toward his face. "We just got an emergency call from the *Gazette* office. Max Biddleman says someone's trying to break in."

This time Bristol didn't offer for me to come along, and I didn't ask. I just took a seat in the back of the cruiser, and nobody objected.

* * *

Max was standing on the sidewalk in front of the *Gazette* office when we arrived, a bloody rag—it looked like part of a t-shirt—wrapped tightly around his hand. I scrambled out of the car to talk to him.

"Stay here," Bristol ordered both of us. He and Sheffey entered the dark *Gazette* office, guns drawn.

"Are you all right?" I asked Max.

He grimaced, looking down at his hand. "I'll be fine." Then he frowned. "What are you doing here?"

I shifted a bit uneasily. "I was with Bristol when the call came in. I just wanted to make sure you were okay."

His expression changed from confusion to one of knowing. "Rennie, I told you to stay away from the Hallacy—"

"Office is clear." Bristol reappeared at the *Gazette*'s front door, his gun holstered again.

Max nodded, still glaring at me.

"I asked her to help out on the Hallacy case. She's the best witness I've got, Max," Bristol said quietly. He'd obviously picked up on the enormous quantity of tension between Max and me.

"Now, you want to tell me what happened here?" An effective change of the subject from Bristol. He was good at that too.

Max took a deep breath and let it out slowly, an attempt to pull himself together enough to think clearly. "I was in the back, working. I...I must have dozed off or something."

I opened my mouth to ask if he'd been sleeping in his office again, but Max stared me down so I stayed quiet. For whatever reason, he didn't want anyone to know he was essentially living at the office. Another odd quirk in his behavior.

"Next thing I know, I hear the sound of glass breaking. I thought I'd dreamed it at first. But then I heard noises, quiet ones, like someone trying to sneak around. So I went to check it out."

I felt more than heard Bristol's disapproval. "And then?" Bristol asked.

"Tripped over something, and fell on some glass." Max held up his wrapped hand. "Surprised the guy, who ran past me and out the back door."

"Did you get a good look at him?" Bristol pulled a notebook and pencil out of his jacket.

Max shook his head. "No, it's dark in the back of the office. The streetlight in the alley behind us burned out months ago, and I had the lights off inside...except in my office, of course." He shifted his weight from foot to foot. I knew he was lying, Bristol probably did too. If any lights had been on in the office, they would have been visible from the outside of the building. Why would anyone break in if it looked like someone was still inside?

"Sheriff." Sheffey stood in the doorway, holding a plastic evidence bag with a rock, probably the size of both my fists and smooth on all the edges, inside. "I found this just inside the back door, near some broken glass. Could be how the intruder gained access to the office."

Bristol looked to us. "Does this belong here? Use it to prop open the back door or something?"

Max and I shook our heads.

"All right, Max. Sheffey will help you get that window in the back door boarded up." Bristol looked back toward Sheffey who nodded. "I'm going to take Rennie back to her car so she can get home."

I stepped a little closer to Max. "You should really have someone take a look at that hand. It could have glass in it, and you might need stitches."

Max jerked his arm toward his chest protectively, like I was going to poke at it. Then he tried to soften his action with words. "Thanks, Rennie. I'll take care of it."

I nodded at him, still frowning, though. I followed Bristol back to the cruiser. We got in and he pointed the car in the direction of his office, where I'd left the BMW.

"Something's wrong with Max," I said.

At the same time, Bristol said, "What's the story with Max?"

See, that's what I loved about being around Bristol. Great minds, and all of that.

"I don't know," I answered his question. "He's been sleeping at the office, I know that for sure."

"Why?"

"I thought it might be a disagreement between him and his, um, friend." I didn't want to contribute to the Morrisville rumor mill with my speculations about Max's love life.

"I know he's gay, Rennie," Bristol said.

I let out a breath of relief. "I wasn't sure for the longest time. Then just little things here and there…" I paused. "Do you know who he is involved with?"

"Yes," Bristol said.

"Nothing gets by you." I waited for him to elaborate, to give me a name.

"What else have you noticed?" he asked instead.

I gritted my teeth at Bristol's ability to keep things to himself. Though it was the right thing to do in this circumstance, it irritated the nosy reporter in me to no end. "He's been seen over at the high school a few times."

Bristol nodded, giving no indication whether that was useful information or not.

"He assigned Johnny Mac and me to a story at the Parkmueller house."

A streetlight illuminated the interior of the car enough for me to see Bristol's mouth pulling upward. "I'm surprised that house hasn't broken open at the seams."

"Or the second story fallen into the basement," I added.

He pulled into a parking space next to my car. "Anything else?"

I shrugged. "You know he assigned the Hallacy story to Arnie Ledbetter. I mean, it would have been one thing for Max to take it for himself. He's the editor, but he still writes a lot. I would have understood that." I still would have been hurt, but probably less so. "But to assign it to Arnie?" I shook my head. "It's like hoping the full story never comes out."

Bristol suddenly went very still next to me, and I realized what I'd said.

I turned to face him, stricken. "Listen, I didn't mean it that way. Max has been acting weird, yes, but not killed-somebody-weird."

"How do you define killed-somebody-weird?" Bristol asked.

I raked my hands through my hair. "I don't know. But Max didn't do it, he didn't kill Doc Hallacy. He has no reason to."

"That we know of," Bristol pointed out.

"What about the break-in tonight? Did he do that too?"

"He could have. Wouldn't have been too hard."

"Why?"

"I don't know, Rennie. It's just another angle I'll have to pursue."

My thoughts were scattered far and wide by the direction this conversation had taken. Suddenly an idea fell into place. "Max couldn't have killed Hallacy," I said with renewed confidence. "He called me on my cell phone right when you guys first got to the pharmacy. He was already in the office, watching everything from the window."

"How do you know he was even in the office? He could have called you from a cell phone."

"Check the phone records, Bristol. You can do that, right? He didn't do it." I pushed the car door open and got out, disgusted with Bristol for this line of questioning and myself for falling into it.

"I have to check it out, Rennie. I like Max as much as anybody, but it's my job."

"Yeah, well, what about all the others you could be checking out?" I demanded.

"Like?" He raised his eyebrows.

I scrambled madly for an answer. "Like…Kitty Alexander, for example."

Bristol made a face.

"People have been killed over lesser things than parking spaces, Bristol. And what about Jenny?"

"Jenny Sturgeon?" Bristol's voice raised in disbelief.

"I'm not saying she did it, but she knows something. I saw her outside your office yesterday and she was acting strangely. When I tried to ask her—"

"The girl is grieving, Rennie. Give her a break."

"What did she inherit, Bristol?"

He sighed.

"Come on, tell me."

"Nothing much. The rest of her college tuition and the use of his house, rent-free, until she graduates."

"Ha," I said pointedly.

"He was already paying for her college, Rennie, and I don't think living in his house for a couple years is motive enough for murder."

"As much of a motive as Max's strange behavior."

"Rennie, we're going to follow up on all the angles we can think of, okay?" Bristol said. "I'm not so anxious to catch this killer that I'll knowingly put the wrong person in jail. But sometimes, sometimes you're forced to look at people you know in a new way. It isn't easy, but it's the only way to try and make sense of things." The dome light in the car left his eyes in shadow, but I felt the intensity of his gaze upon me. I knew we weren't just talking about Max anymore, but I didn't know what he was saying about us—not that such a thing existed—and I suddenly felt too weary to try and puzzle it out.

"Good night, Bristol."

"Night, Rennie."

I slammed the car door shut on his words. He waited to leave until I got in my car and pulled away without any trouble. That was just the kind of person he was and part of what made everything so damn complicated.

ELEVEN

"Which one you looking for?" Tessa Sturgeon exhaled cigarette smoke with her words, holding one skinny arm close to her waist like she was hugging herself.

This morning I woke up in a foul mood. I couldn't quite shake the vague, gnawing sense of discontent that had stuck with me ever since my conversation with Bristol last night. I knew Bristol was just doing his job and he would do it well, but he was forced to follow evidence and the direction it pointed, which happened to be straight at Max, for the moment. Therefore, I'd added visiting Jenny Sturgeon to my to-do list for the day. I'd told Bristol the truth; I didn't think she'd done anything wrong, but boy, unless I was way off in reading her, she sure knew somebody who had.

"I'm looking for Jenny. Is she here?"

Tessa nodded, frowning. "She's a good one. What do you want with her?"

"Just to talk."

She stubbed out her cigarette on the porch ledge and flicked the butt into the bushes. "I know you. You don't want to talk, just stir up trouble." I'd seen this woman waiting tables at Ruby's a hundred times, but I'd never put it together that Tess at Ruby's was Tessa Sturgeon until now, when I saw her on her back porch in her Ruby's uniform. Sometimes the investigative reporter part of me didn't come so naturally.

I gritted my teeth in an effort to keep from saying something to defend myself. Somehow I thought that might only make things worse. "It'll only take a few minutes."

She stared at me for a long moment, then nodded. "Go on. She's inside."

I hesitated, thinking she'd put out her cigarette to go in the house with me. Instead, she pulled out her pack of menthols and lit up another one. "Watch your wallet," she mumbled.

"Excuse me?" I asked, not certain I'd heard her correctly.

"The younger ones. Some of them are pretty slippery." She eyed my bag. "You should really have a zipper to close that thing. They can get under those Velcro flaps like they aren't even there."

I stared at her. She sounded like the caretaker at Juvenile Hall rather than the mother of these delinquents.

"And if you take your coat off, don't leave it laying around. One of them, I think it's Julia, is real fond of leather."

"Are you serious?" I asked.

She shrugged. "If you like that coat, I am."

Muttering a prayer of thanks for my own crazy-in-a-different-way mother, I headed past Tessa into her house.

The Sturgeon house was as spectacularly chaotic as I ever imagined it to be, and way more clean. The front door opened into a tiny living room. The carpeting was thin and worn but viciously vacuumed. Children, from infant size in carriers to toddlers and pre-schoolers, their little behinds fat with diapers, filled the room. Most of them were watching the old color television, one with knobs and an antenna, parked on an old piano bench in a corner. A dancing character of some kind (static made it hard to see clearly) sang about loving your friends and eating vegetables or some other such thing. I did a quick head count and figured there were at least eight kids in here, but they kept moving around and some of them looked too much alike for me to be sure I'd counted correctly. These had to be children of the original Sturgeon girls, cousins to each other rather than siblings. There were just too many who were too close in age for it to be anything else.

I headed past them, wrinkling my nose at the scent of an overdue diaper, and came to a small dining room. The table had been removed at some point. Only chairs, a variety of shapes and sizes, remained, lining either side of the room along the wall, making it look more like a bus station than a dining room. Either everyone had a TV tray stored somewhere, or they were really good at balancing meals on their laps. Just beyond the room, through a swinging door, I heard a whoop of laughter and the clatter of dishes, so I kept moving.

Once through the swinging door, I found myself in the kitchen, the largest room I'd seen so far, and no less crowded. Three women, looking nearly identical, especially in their weariness, bustled around the kitchen, scooping eggs onto plates, filling bottles, and stacking dirty dishes in the sink.

"Something I can help you with, love?" a male voice asked, close to my elbow.

I looked down and found Milo Sturgeon sitting at the kitchen table, a newspaper spread before him and a glass of what I would bet to be vodka and orange juice at his fingertips. He was rumored to have once been a good-looking guy, and I could see the remnants easily in my first up-close look at him. The heavy shiny black hair he'd passed on to Jenny and all the other sisters still remained thick on him, though shot with silver now. His blue eyes were still bright, but rimmed with red and watery. Somehow, I'd missed seeing him on my first glance in the room. He'd been lost in the swirling activity of his daughters, something he was probably long accustomed to.

"I'm looking for Jenny," I said.

"Oh. Well, sit down first." He kicked a chair out toward me. "Have a drink with me." He smiled at me, and I found myself smiling back. No wonder he had twelve kids. His charm was undeniable.

"No, Pa." One of the daughters turned from her work at the counter to grasp me on the shoulder and steer me away. "Jenny's upstairs." The woman gave me a little push toward a door I hadn't noticed in the corner.

"Thanks," I said.

She nodded at me, a lock of her dark hair falling against her face. The magnificent blue eyes she'd gotten from her father were lined with worry and exhaustion. I wondered how many of the kids out in the other room were hers. She turned back toward the counter and started filling bottles again.

I moved past her toward the door. As I opened it, I heard Milo Sturgeon say in a hurt tone, "Why'd you do that? I just wanted a little company."

One of the daughters, presumably the one who'd spoken to me, answered him with patient exasperation. "Because, Pa, you can't have company without charming the pants off someone, and we don't need any more kids around here."

Swallowing back a mortified giggle, I hurried up the stairs. I reached the top and discovered the second floor was one giant room, running the length and width of the entire downstairs. Beds were set up along the walls, six on each side, dormitory style. At the moment, though, only a few were occupied. I spotted Jenny at the other end of the room, stretched on a bed by the one window in the room, reading from what looked like a textbook. I walked toward her, but only got a few feet before another girl, identical to Jenny except a little shorter and wearing a nose ring, got off her bed and stood in front of me in the aisle between the rows of beds.

"Nice jacket." She stroked the edge of my sleeve appreciatively.

"Thanks, Julia." I watched her eyes widen in surprise. "But I intend to keep it."

She let out a loud dramatic sigh, and then stomped back to her bed. "I don't always take things," she muttered under her breath.

"Talk to your mother, then," I said.

I kept going until I reached Jenny's bed, where she'd stopped reading to watch me approach, her eyes bright with fear.

"I don't have anything to say to you." Jenny got up and tried to dart around me in the narrow aisle.

I caught her arm. "I just have a few questions."

She shook her head wildly.

"I don't think you did anything wrong," I whispered. By now, I could feel Julia and the other two girls in the room watching us. Weren't they supposed to be in school? Why, for heaven's sake, was Jenny still living here when she now had her own place to go to?

"I don't have anything to say to you," she said in a trembling voice. Her eyes watched something behind me, most likely her sisters. "Now let me go."

An idea struck, and I took a stab in the dark. "If you don't talk to me, I'm going to start saying how wonderful it is that Doc left you his house to live in for a couple years," I whispered. The only reason I could think of for her to be still living here was she didn't want them to know about Doc's house, wanted it to be hers alone, a seemingly foreign concept in this family. She could probably get away with keeping it secret for awhile, too. We hadn't run a story on Doc's will in the *Gazette*, mainly because I didn't want to tell Max I'd attended. He hadn't sent Arnie to cover it, nor would any of the Sturgeons likely hear of Jenny's good fortune through town gossip. They were too often the cause of gossip to be included in the regular bouts of whispering.

Tears filled Jenny's enormous blue eyes, and I felt horrible. She nodded.

"Is there a place we can talk?" I asked in a normal voice, letting go of her arm.

"This way," she mumbled. Jenny led me past her sisters, down the stairs, through the kitchen and out the back door to the gravel driveway.

She turned on me. "Do you know what's it like to never have any privacy? To never have anything that's yours alone?" she demanded. Her fists were clenched and shaking at her sides.

As an only child, no, I guess I didn't. "Listen, I don't want to take anything away from you. I just want to talk."

She relaxed slightly. "So you won't tell them about Doc's house?"

I shook my head. "Why are you hiding it? They're going to notice when you move out."

"I'm not moving out." She wiped her sleeve across her teary face. "I just go there when I need to study or I want some private time. Sometimes I sneak out at night and come back in the morning. Otherwise…"

"Otherwise, they'll know," I finished. "And then it won't be just yours anymore."

She shook her head. "You don't get it." She tilted her face toward the sky and gave a shaky laugh. "We're scavengers, all of us. We've learned to live that way. If I let them into Doc's house, things'd start to go missing. A vase here or a couch there. And it's not mine to keep or give away. They'd pick it clean."

"But you wouldn't because…" I prompted, genuinely trying to understand this.

She dropped her gaze to me, now glaring. "Because I know the difference between right and wrong."

I raised an eyebrow.

She sighed. "Doc Hallacy caught me stealing, the first week I worked there. A lipstick." She smiled and looked down at her feet. "Blush Rose. He told me if he ever caught me doing it again, he'd tan my hide and then fire me." Her smile wilted a bit, and her tears returned. "Then he sold me everything at a 75% discount, and for my birthday, he gave me that stupid lipstick." She looked up at me, eyes shining. "I never even used it. Just hid it away so the other girls wouldn't get at it, the one thing that was mine only."

I stepped toward her, touched her on the arm. "I promise I won't say anything about the house, but I need you to tell me the truth. The other day when I asked you about Doc Hallacy's murder, you acted like you knew something."

She shifted a little from foot to foot, an automatic protest springing from her lips. "No, I…I don't know what happened that morning," she said, looking down.

"No, but you suspect something. All I'm asking you to do is share that with me," I urged. "The wrong man may end up getting arrested if you don't speak up."

Her eyes teared up again. "But they're my family," she whispered.

Oh, Lord. "What happened, Jenny?" I prompted gently.

She turned her back to me. For a moment, I thought she had decided to keep her silence, then she said, over her shoulder, "You know the break-in a few months ago?"

"The teenagers? Yeah, I know about that."

"I think that was my fault."

"How?" I asked, astounded.

"My brother, Jamie, was asking me one night about—"

"Wait, you have a brother?" I asked, confused. Everyone always talked about the Sturgeon girls. Nobody'd ever mentioned

122

the Sturgeon boys. Did that mean there were actually thirteen, or more, Sturgeon children?

"I have two brothers. I'm the ninth girl, but the tenth kid. My brother Jamie is a year old than me. My brother Jessie is a year younger."

"Don't you have sisters named Jamie and Jessie too?"

She shrugged. "Pa wanted all girls, I guess."

"Okay, so you said Jamie was asking you about something…"

"Yeah. He said he was worried about me working there by myself with just an old man. What if someone tried to rob the place?" She shook her head. "I should have known, like Jamie would have cared what happened to me. There are eleven others just like me."

"No." I touched her shoulder. "You are a unique Sturgeon, as far as I know."

She gave me a weak smile, and then continued. "So I told him not to worry. That I was only there for a few hours a day, and there were security cameras and everything."

All the pieces suddenly fit together in my mind, and my heart slipped a few notches for her. "A few days later, there was a break-in," I finished.

She nodded. "They never told me it was them, or anything, but the newspaper came out with the article saying one of them was wearing a track t-shirt." She sighed. "Jessie had just been bragging how he'd stolen a shirt from one of the varsity runners."

Oh, boy. "All right, Jenny, you need to tell Sheriff Bristol about this."

She stepped back from me, her eyes wild. "I can't. They'll kill me. You saw what they did to Doc and—"

"Jenny, no, I don't think they killed Doc," I said.

"What?" She calmed down enough to look at me.

"I don't think they killed Doc," I said again, but it was clear she didn't believe me. "Look, I was there, the one who found him, all right? There wasn't anything messed up or taken as far as I could see. If your brothers had been there looking for drugs, they'd have just shoved everything they could grab into a bag and run, particularly if they'd just killed a man." 'Course, they could have been too scared by what they'd done and just run. After hearing the way Jenny described her family, though, I didn't think they would miss such an opportunity to make life a little easier for themselves, either by selling the drugs or using them themselves.

She nodded slowly. Apparently, my theory made sense to her. Unfortunately, it didn't help me in the slightest. By eliminating Jenny Sturgeon and her brothers, it only further sharpened the arrow pointing at Max.

"I still want you to talk to Bristol," I said. "He'll figure it out eventually anyway, and this way, maybe he'll go easier on your brothers." I doubted it, but Jenny didn't deserve to be carrying around this kind of burden. "I'll even go with you, if you want."

She shook her head and squared her shoulders. "No, I'll do it." She sighed. "Besides, Mama always says nothing but jail will straighten the two of them out anyway."

I fought the urge not to shake my head in disbelief. "Well, let me know if you change your mind. You're doing the right thing. And..." I hesitated. "Doc would be proud of you for it."

She nodded, tears trembling on her eyelashes again, and then turned and headed into her house. I circled around the side of the Sturgeon house to get back to my car parked on the street.

Now what? I was all out of leads. Despite what I'd told Bristol, I didn't really think Kitty Alexander could have done it. She might have chipped a nail while hammering that final blow toward Doc. Definitely not her style, but whose style was it? I didn't know, and with Doc's death already more than three days old and Max looking more and more suspicious, I was running out of time to find out.

* * *

I went home after visiting Jenny, to collect my thoughts and a notebook. In my haste to get to her this morning, I'd rushed out of the apartment without one, which meant I had nothing more than a receipt or two for writing down my thoughts, in case I happened to come up with a doozy. Hey, it happens every now and again.

I pulled around the corner and into the alley next to my mother's house in time to see her slipping out of the house and hurrying toward her car.

I put down the window. "Mom," I called out.

She jumped visibly.

"Where are you going?" I asked. She was dressed again in her Sunday clothes, a turquoise blouse with a matching skirt.

She lifted her chin defiantly, but her eyes wouldn't meet mine. "I have some errands to run."

Blame it on poor sleep, a bad mood, or just lack of coffee, but I couldn't let it go. "Like the errand you ran all day on Saturday?" I asked.

Color rose in her face, but she didn't take the bait. "Yes," she answered. Then she continued past me, like that was the end of the conversation.

I put the car in park and climbed out. "What, have you got a hot date or something at..." I checked my watch. "...10:17 in the morning?"

She turned in her low heels and crunched over the gravel to where I stood near the BMW. "Don't you say that." Her finger jabbed at the air in front of me. "I won't have you disrespecting me or your father in that way."

"Disrespecting?" Blood buzzed in my ears. "Me? How about lying to me about where you've been or where you're going? You're the one who is disrespecting—"

"I don't owe you any explanation for my behavior or my whereabouts at any time. You hear me, Irene Mae?" She stepped closer, her teeth clenched and the words just barely escaping, just like she'd done when I'd thrown tantrums in the grocery store as a kid. My mother apparently still worried about what people might think if they overheard. "I'm an adult."

Lord help me, I should have let it go. "An adult, yes. An adult with a major illness, right, Mom? Which one is it today? Maybe you'll get lucky and catch Ebola and cancer at the same time. They'll cancel each other out."

She jerked, as if I'd slapped her. "Who asked you to come back here, Rennie, and stick your nose where it doesn't belong?" She clutched her hand bag tighter. "Certainly not me."

Stung, I pulled back a little. She marched past me toward the garage. Regret left a bitter taste in my mouth. "Mom, wait." I chased after her.

"Rennie, I don't have time to talk to you right now, nor do I want to. Is that clear?" Her tone was clipped. She raised the garage door without asking for my help as she normally did.

I followed her into the dim garage. "Mom, I'm sorry. I...I didn't mean what I said."

She paused in the act of climbing into her car to look back at me. "You should be sorry, Rennie. I've never heard such horrible words from you."

"I said I'm sorry!"

"Sometimes that isn't enough, and you know it." With that, she got into her car, closed the door, and started the engine, forcing me out of the garage for a clean gasp of air. She pulled out into the alleyway and headed toward the street, without so much as backward glance at me.

I wanted to scream. Instead, I put the garage door down, hopping up until I could reach the edge to yank it, so she'd have to make noise when she came back. Then I could come down and try to apologize again.

With a groan, I climbed up to my apartment to get my notebook, and, of course, when I got there, my phone was ringing. I snatched it off the hook.

"Hello?" I demanded.

Nothing but silence on the other end.

"Hello? Who is this?"

No response except breathing and then a faint click.

I jabbed the off-button on the phone, which wasn't nearly as satisfying as slamming it down on a cradle used to be, and then dialed Jeff's home number. I still had it memorized; after all, it used to be my number. He and Maria were living in our old townhouse until they found a place of their own. Maybe he was finding that a house cost more than he expected, but too bad. I wasn't going to put up with the harassment one second longer. That was like the tenth hang-up I'd had in three days. If I called now, I could just leave an angry message rather than having to speak with either one of them. As far as I knew, they both should be at work. 'Course, that meant I'd have to suffer through more hang-ups from him calling from work or his cell before he got home to check his messages. Oh, well.

On the third ring at their home number, Maria answered. "Hello?"

I gritted my teeth. "Maria, it's Rennie. Tell Jeff to stop calling here."

"Rennie." Was it my imagination or did her voice get a little colder? "That money doesn't belong to you. He has every right to ask for it back."

Anger exploded in me, tightening my grip on the phone until the plastic creaked in my ear. "No, I have a legal right to it, according to all the papers he signed. You know, the ones that made him your problem, not mine."

"I told him you would never understand." Her Puerto Rican accent thickened. She was one of those women who, according to my ex-husband, only grew more beautiful and exotic in anger. Damn her and him. "What cold white woman who let her husband go in the first place is going to care about his problems now? I ask him, but he say, oh, no, Maria. I will handle her."

"I didn't let go of him, you...." I paused, trying to calm myself. This wasn't going to turn into the Jerry Springer show, not if I could help it. After all, I had the upper hand here. I'd gotten rid of Jeff but kept his money. She had the reverse problem. It made me wonder if it had been her calling all along, instead of Jeff. "Stop calling me, or I will talk to the police."

"Crazy woman. You called here, or did you forget that already?"

"I mean it, Maria. I'm not giving back any money and his check better damn well be on time."

"Why? You don't need it. Hiding there all alone with your mama and—"

Sounds of a tussle ensued on the other end of the phone.

"Rennie?" Jeff's voice on the other end of the phone, sounding slightly out of breath. In the background, I could hear Maria still shouting. Then it grew muffled as if he'd shut a door somewhere.

"Jeff."

"I'm so glad you called." Fake sincerity sent his voice into Barry White octaves.

"Save it, Jeff. I'm not letting you off the hook with the money."

"But Rennie." His voice immediately shot up into a familiar whine. "We need it."

"Why?" I expected a multitude of excuses to begin, one after another, until he found one he thought I might go for.

Instead, he hesitated. "We're expecting."

My brain was so far afield, I didn't even get it at first. "Expecting what? Another Louis XIV armoire?"

"A baby, Rennie."

Suddenly dizzy, I sat down hard on the couch. Fritzy cried, evidently picking up on my mood. "When?" I said, although I already knew the answer.

"A few weeks."

That was who gets married on a Thursday, three days after finalizing a divorce—people who already have a family on the way

"It's twins, actually." He sounded proud and exhausted. "Maria's home on bed rest, and I'm working from home so I can look after her."

"Twins?" I said weakly. It wasn't just that—two babies where I couldn't even have one. Jeff had actually taken a risk on his career to stay at home and care for his wife. I'd stayed home with a vicious flu once, early in our marriage, and my doctor had wanted me to go to the emergency room. I'd called Jeff at work, and he'd told me to take a cab. To be confronted with direct evidence about how little he'd cared about me in contrast to Maria...I felt sick to my stomach.

"I didn't want to tell you this way," he said.

"Is there any good way?" Tears closed off my throat, and I swallowed hard.

"I am sorry, Rennie," he said.

"Don't worry about it. That's not your job anymore, right?" I got up and grabbed a handful of napkins off the breakfast bar to wipe my face.

Jeff remained quiet for a few moments. Then he said, "About the money...."

I groaned. "Jeff, you haven't changed. You're so damn focused on one thing, you tromp on everything else to get to it."

"Well, what do you want me to do?" he demanded. "Everything's so expensive up here, and Maria wants this four bedroom house in the suburbs. She wants the kids to have their own rooms."

"They're not even born yet!"

"I know, but Rennie," he lowered his voice to a whisper, "she won't leave me alone about it."

"You married her. So I guess that's your problem, not mine."

"Why do you always have to be so cold?" he whined.

Even knowing our marriage had probably been a mistake and I wouldn't take him back if he crawled, his words still hurt. I stiffened. "As you once told me, it's the facts that matter, not the feelings. The facts say the money is mine."

"But you don't need it. You can't tell me your mother is charging you rent."

"It doesn't matter, Jeff. It's the principle of the thing."

"Come on, Rennie, please," he wheedled. "You don't know what she's like. It used to be so much easier with you."

Of course, it was, you idiot. Because I trusted you, and she knows better. "I'll think about," I said finally, trying to remind myself there were innocent children involved. Children who would have been related to my son. I clamped down on the grief that threatened to swell up against me then.

He exhaled loudly in relief. "Thank you, Rennie. You don't

know how—"

"I didn't say I agreed to it, Jeff," I warned. "Only that I'd think about it. So don't push your luck, and stop calling me."

"I don't think it was unreasonable to call you once." He sounded offended.

"How about all the other times you call and hang up, then?"

"I don't know what you're talking about, but I think we're beyond the juvenile here." He sniffed, his composure restored by what he considered my capitulation to his demands.

"Check with Maria, then. Because somebody's been calling here at all hours of the night."

"Rennie, she doesn't even have your number. It's programmed on my cell." He sounded exasperated.

Jeff was never without his cell, even if he didn't answer it. So, if he hadn't made the calls—as despicable as he was, I could sense his genuine confusion—who had? The problem would have been easily solved if I had just purchased Caller ID, but I hadn't, in order to save money. It'd never occurred to me to *69 after one of the calls because I thought it was Jeff.

"Rennie, are you still there?" he asked.

"Yeah, I'm here. We'll talk more later about this." My thoughts were scattered by this new revelation. I had enough sense to add, "I'll call you, don't call me."

"Fine, whatever you say, Rennie," he said with irritation in his voice. Then he hung up.

I turned the phone off and hung it back up on the wall. I couldn't think who else would be calling me and hanging up...except Margene Bristol. I tried to remember if any of the calls had come in while I knew she was somewhere else, like the Garden Show, but there'd been so many calls by now, and I'd deleted the hang-ups on my machine.

Only thing to do now was wait for it to happen again. This time, I would be ready for her.

TWELVE

It was almost two o'clock by the time I gave up waiting for the phone to ring, ate some lunch, and headed over to First Episcopal. Father Dan had told me not to hurry, that he would be there all day, but I still felt bad about making him wait around for me. One more pile of guilt on top of a growing mountain of it.

"Rennie, I hope you don't mind me asking, but are you okay?" Father Dan's worried face leaned a little closer. From the few times I'd met him, I liked Father Dan. He just had this sense of peace about him, something that made it so tempting to confess anything and everything you've ever done for a possible taste of that same peace. He was like none of the other pastors I'd known. He was young, probably only ten years older than me, with a pretty wife and two little boys.

I sighed, making the newsletter ideas, written on scraps of paper by various congregation members with illegible handwriting, flutter and shift on the desk in front of me. Father Dan had settled me at an empty desk in the open secretarial area outside his private office. Now, on his way back from the copier, he'd evidently caught me staring off into space again. I couldn't quite keep the concentration I needed, after all that had happened this morning.

Depends on how you define okay. A client of mine, a friend sort of, is probably under suspicion of murder, I threatened a girl into talking to me, my mother won't speak to me, my ex-husband has turned out to be a decent husband to his second wife, they're expecting twins now, and I think I'm in love with the sheriff, the married sheriff.

I considered actually saying all of that out loud. It might have felt better than continuing to haul it around inside me. Seeing Father Dan struggle to keep a blank face probably would have been priceless. But it affected too many people outside of me, and my comfort wasn't worth the loss of theirs.

"I had a fight with my mother," I said. That was bothering me, albeit only as a portion of the whole picture. Still, it might be good to get the Father's opinion on this safer, but no less troubling issue.

"What happened?" he asked.

I told him the gory details, including my own horrible words. "I'm not even sure what to say when I see her again," I confessed at the end. "I think maybe I should move farther away. It was never my plan to stay that close forever anyway, just till I got my job situation worked out and I knew she'd be okay on her own. She clearly doesn't want me around anymore."

Father Dan shook his head. "You're two adults living in close proximity to one another. Her illness only increases the sense of responsibility you feel for her."

"So what's wrong with that? I am my brother's keeper, right?"

"Right. But everyone must make their own choices. If she wants to date and not tell you about it, she probably has her reasons." He hesitated and then continued. "The same way, I'm sure you have your reasons for telling me only part of what's bothering you."

I smiled, but said nothing.

"Talk to your mother when she gets home. Make sure she knows that you're okay with whatever she decides, as long as it's healthy for her. And Rennie," he said, looking over the top of his glasses at me, "she's still a competent adult, so she gets to decide what's healthy, not you. Just because you don't like a choice she makes doesn't mean it's bad for her."

"Even if she's dating some biker guy from Springfield with three ex-wives and a criminal record?" I imagined my mother's turquoise skirt billowing out on either side of her legs as she clutched some burly man on the back of Harley.

"Is he reformed?" Father Dan asked immediately.

I laughed. "All right. Point taken."

"I'll leave you to your work, then." He stood and started pulling his chair back to his office. He paused and turned back toward me. "Rennie, I'm always here if you want to talk about whatever else is on your mind. You've got a confidentiality agreement with me without even having to sign any papers."

"Thanks, I appreciate it, but—"

"Whatever's bothering isn't something you feel comfortable discussing with a minister," he finished for me. He shook his head. "You'd be surprised by what I hear."

I raised my eyebrows.

"Not that you'll ever hear it yourself, part of that confidentiality agreement I mentioned," he said quickly. "Just remember there's no sin too great for the Lord to forgive."

Even still, I thought I might be testing the Lord's limits, so I let Father Dan return to his office without saying more.

* * *

A little after seven, I finished writing up the newsletter articles. On my way out the door, I stuck my head in Father Dan's office to let him know I'd return tomorrow after Doc Hallacy's funeral to make final adjustments to the layout. Graphic design was a little out of my element, but First Episcopal had a computer program that made creating a newsletter layout relatively simple.

I stepped outside into a gray and dreary evening, the early sunshine of the day devoured by clouds and a sopping rain. The farmers would be pleased. I started to drive home, intending to talk with my mother as Father Dan had recommended, but as I turned back onto Main Street, I passed the *Gazette* office. Despite Father Dan's words of letting people make their own choices, I had to stop.

I pulled open the front door, trying to keep the wind and rain from blowing in with me. Arnie Ledbetter was the only one out front. He was sitting at *my desk*, his balding head tipped down in concentration as he hunted and pecked *my story* on an ancient typewriter he'd dug up from somewhere. The red bowtie at his throat bobbed up and down as he spelled each word aloud to find the right keys.

"Where's Max?" I brushed off the rain clinging to the sleeves of my leather jacket.

Arnie looked up. A slow grin spread across his face. "Well, if it isn't the big city writer. Heard you got the Parkmueller story."

"Yeah, and it's done already." I stared pointedly at the line or two of copy on the paper sticking out of his typewriter. "Now where's Max?"

Arnie scowled. "In back. He's on the phone, I think. You should knock first."

I headed toward Max's office, ignored Arnie's warning, and barged right in.

Max looked up. He was indeed on the phone, his now neatly bandaged hand holding the receiver up to his ear. "I'm going to have to call you back," he said. He hung without waiting for the other person's response. "Rennie, I'm not giving you back the Hallacy—"

I brushed his words away. "It's not about that." I dropped onto the sofa in front of his desk. "I don't even know if I should be doing this. But I thought you should know."

Max leaned forward in his chair in anticipation of what I was going to say.

"Bristol thinks you're hiding something, and so do I."

Max's face evened out, blocking all signs of emotion. "Rennie…."

I held up my hand to stop his protest. "If you don't want to tell me, I don't care." I paused. "Actually, I do care because I didn't think there was anything worth lying this much about, and it's going to get you in trouble." I took a deep breath. "Bristol thinks you're somehow involved in Hallacy's murder."

"I see," Max said.

I stared at him. This couldn't be good. No shout of denial, no anger mottling his face as I'd seen on so many occasions, no declaration of innocence.

"Thanks for your time, Rennie. I do appreciate you stopping by." Max picked up the phone again and began to dial.

I reached across the desk and slammed down the disconnect button. "Did you not hear what I'm saying to you? You could end up being a murder suspect. Trust me, I've been there. It's not all that HBO and John Grisham novels make it out to be."

Max laid the receiver back down carefully in the cradle and folded his hands on his desk. He appeared to be struggling with keeping his temper. "Thank you, Rennie. You can go now. Your last check will be in the mail tomorrow."

I stood, the blood rushing away from my head, leaving me slightly dizzy. "You're firing me?" I'd never been fired before, not even been threatened with it…except from Max, of course.

"I no longer have need of your services." He rearranged the papers on his desk, keeping his eyes away from mine.

"You're firing me for warning you?" I stared at him in disbelief.

"No," he shouted, startling me. "I'm firing you for not being able to stay away from the Hallacy story. I gave it to Arnie."

I nodded, my vision blurry with tears generated as much by anger as hurt. "I'm sure you did that for good reasons, right?"

He didn't respond.

"Go to hell, Max." I spun on my heel and threw open Max's office door, nearly knocking an eavesdropping Arnie on his skinny butt.

"I'm already there," I thought I heard Max say as I stormed off.

"Oh, no," I shouted. "You wait until Bristol gets done with you. When everyone in town thinks you did it even if you didn't. When every secret you ever hoped was buried comes out on the front page. Then we'll talk about hell, Max."

I rushed out into the rain, the warm drops mixing with my tears. At least no one would notice I'd been crying again. As long as they overlooked the swollen lids and red eyes I had going on, that is.

I pointed my car toward home, intending to confront my mother to polish off this crappy day, but in a weak moment, I made a left instead of a right and found myself in the parking lot of the Sheriff's Office. Warm air churned out of the car's vents, drying my hair and my face. The unchanging rhythm of the windshield wipers soothed me. I sat there, car running, for fifteen minutes or more, trying to decide what to do. Much as I hated to help build a case against Max, Bristol deserved to know what had just happened. I'd accused Max of hiding something and he'd practically admitted it by firing me. Firing an employee, even a freelancer, for getting too close to the truth could be important information for Bristol. That wasn't why I was here, though, and I knew it. I wanted comfort. I wanted someone to hold me and say that everything was going to be okay. I wanted someone to say

Max was an idiot for firing me, that I hadn't deserved it, and that Jeffrey Michael was still a jackass even if he was now a better husband to somebody else. Mostly, I just wanted Bristol.

I had my hand on the car door handle, ready to push open the door when I saw the three of them. I recognized Bristol immediately, though his hat shielded most of his face. The other two, smaller and wrapped from head to knees in bright plastic raincoats, took me a second. The shortest one bounced to a waiting minivan with the enthusiasm of a child and the other...well, Bristol stopped when he saw me sitting there, and so did the remaining mystery figure. My heart fell. Margene. It had to be. She lifted her hood back to see what her husband was looking at, and the smile faded from her face when she saw me.

"Everything okay?" Bristol mouthed to me from outside the car.

I nodded, plastered a smile on my face, and put the car in reverse. Going to eat a family dinner, at Ruby's Cafe probably, while Bristol took an hour off duty. I couldn't and wouldn't interrupt that.

I pulled out of the parking lot in a mad hurry, hoping it hadn't looked as pathetic as it felt. I didn't know what to do. I couldn't go home and face my mother, not yet. I couldn't go to the *Gazette*. Definitely not to the Sheriff's Office or Ruby's. I had no place to go. That's how I ended up out at the lake, which created more trouble than if I'd gone to all the other places I'd thought of. Of course, I didn't know that at the time.

THIRTEEN

Not counting the visit to Marty Halpern's house yesterday, I hadn't been to the lake in years, probably not since I left for college. It had been a favorite spot of my dad's. For fishing, swimming, family picnics, you name it. Somewhere out here, probably at the marina or maybe a rented boathouse, my dad still had a fishing boat, unless Mom had sold it. He'd called it *The Minnow*, something I hadn't gotten until I was much older and we had cable for Nick at Night reruns. I'd have to ask my mom about the fate of *The Minnow*, if she would speak to me again.

I stayed huddled in my car, watching the gray water grow little white caps from the wind and feeling more miserable and alone than I had even when Jeff left. It had been out here, at Lake Morris, that I'd had my first meltdown over a boy. Adam Fisher had asked Marissa Clark to the freshman homecoming dance instead of me (she was rumored to French and I didn't). I'd wanted to stay home and sulk, but Dad had dragged me out onto the boat with him to share the last beautiful fall day with him. Now I was glad I'd spent the day with him. At the time, though, not so much.

"What if I go and I'm the only one without a date?" I'd wailed, probably scaring away any fish in a five mile radius.

"You might be," my dad had said, apparently undisturbed by the prospect of my imminent social doom.

"What if I'm always the only one without a date? What if there's an odd number of people in the world and I'm the leftover?" I was fourteen, prone to hormone-induced tantrums and addicted to drama.

My dad had set aside his fishing pole and squeezed my hand. "Rennie, sweetheart, you can't spend the rest of your life trying to win the approval of everyone else. Why would you want to pretend to be someone or something you're not just so you're not alone?"

"Duh. So I'm not alone."

"But then they don't really like you, they like who you're pretending to be."

"Close enough," I muttered.

He'd laughed then, I remembered that, and gave me sideways hug, the best possible in the cramped and unsteady space of *The Minnow*. "I like you, just the way you are, kiddo."

"You have to like me, you're my dad."

"No, no." He'd shaken his head and picked up his fishing pole again. "I have to love you. The liking thing can be sort of touch and go, these days. If I like you, other people will too. Just be yourself and give it some time."

Except being me seems only to get me into more trouble, these days, Dad, I thought. In that instant, I was mad at him for leaving, for making my mother worry more than she ever had when he was alive, for not being here to smooth out her rough edges, for being absent when I desperately needed the calm words of wisdom I'd ignored as a kid.

"It'd have been nice if you'd stuck around just a little longer," I shouted into the empty interior of the car. I pounded my fist on the steering wheel, hoping it would make me feel better, but it only made the horn bleat and my hand hurt.

I sat there for a long time after that, not realizing how much time had passed until I noticed it was full-on dark outside. I wiped my face, straightened myself up and turned on the car. The dashboard clock glowed 9:07. I had to get back home for Fritzy, if for nothing else. I'd wasted enough time out here on self-pity. It

141

was time to face the music, or, more accurately, the various angry people in town.

I put the car in gear and started to back out across the grass to reach the road again. Headlights flared suddenly in my rearview mirror and I instinctively hit the brakes, though the other car was still some distance off.

Who else would be out here this late at night, in the rain? The car kept coming closer, headed straight for me. A sudden chill danced along my skin, despite the warmth inside my car. Whoever had killed Doc Hallacy was still out there, and maybe not too happy with me for asking questions.

I hit the gas and flew toward the oncoming car to see if they would stop when they saw me coming. If not, I'd try to slip past on one side or the other.

The car kept coming, though more slowly, and finally at the last second, just as I was preparing to whip the steering wheel to the left, red and blue lights flashed on the top of the other car.

I braked hard, sliding a bit in the mud, and let out a breath of relief. It was just Sheffey or Barnes, or maybe even Sheryl, out to bust somebody for trespassing. The lake was technically closed after dark. I put down my window and stuck my head out, blinking in the rain, to see who it was and let them know it was me.

"Rennie!" Barnes's voice was recognizable even over the sound of the heater running and the downpour of rain. He jogged to my side of the car.

"What are you doing here," I started to ask.

"Bristol thought you might be out here. We've been trying to find you." He hesitated. "It's your mom, Rennie. She—"

I didn't wait to hear any more. I gunned the engine, spun around and got back onto the road to town, while Barnes scrambled into his car after me.

As soon as I turned the corner onto my street, I saw red lights, flashing intermittently, painting my mother's house a pale pink. An ambulance sat in the alleyway off of Fairlane, near the gravel parking area in our yard.

My heart flew higher into my throat. What had happened? I pulled off to the side of the road in front of the house, so I didn't block the ambulance, threw the gearshift into park, and ran toward the ambulance. A small crowd of neighbors had appeared, clustered together some distance from the vehicle. I heard my name a few times, but I ignored it. I could only imagine it must have looked much the same here when Mom found Dad in his basement workshop after his heart attack.

My stomach twisted as I rounded the edge of the ambulance and saw my mother inside, lying on a gurney.

Dark blood matted her short gray hair. "Mama," I bleated. Terror for her turned me into a child again.

Hands grabbed at me, pulling me away, and I shoved at them, my eyes only on my mother.

"Rennie," someone said and shook me hard enough I bit my tongue. I dragged my eyes away from my mother to find Sheffey grasping my shoulders.

"We've been looking for you everywhere. We couldn't get through on your cell phone."

"I turned it off," I said through numb lips. I hadn't wanted anyone to disturb my little pity party.

"Bristol was afraid you'd come home to find her gone and panic."

I managed to focus on Sheffey's face. "Is she all right?"

"Your mother's going to be fine. Just a bump on the head. Barnes tried to tell you before you sped off," he said. Just as the words left his mouth, two more squad cars, lights blazing, pulled up behind the first one I hadn't even seen.

"What happened?" I watched Bristol get out of his car and head this way. Something tight in my chest loosened at the sight of him. He paused only momentarily to speak with a mud-splattered Barnes. I must have gotten Barnes good with my tires when I pulled away at the lake.

Sheffey lifted a shoulder. "Don't really have the full story yet. Neighbor noticed something amiss and called us and an ambulance." Only then did I notice Joann Stokes, my mother's neighbor who'd helped look after her before I'd come home, sitting in her leopard skin patterned robe, at my mother's side.

"Rennie, you all right?" Bristol approached us.

I nodded, my head feeling a bit too loose on its axis. "I need to talk to my mom."

"All right now, but just calm down," Sheffey instructed. "She's going to be fine, and she doesn't need to get all worked up again. You know how she…" He stopped, seeing my face tighten.

"You don't have to tell me how she is, Sheffey. She's my mother, damnit." I brushed past him.

I approached the open doors of the ambulance slowly, afraid that if I ran, all my control would disappear. The EMT standing outside in the now drizzling rain greeted me.

"She's doing fine. She has a bump on her head and a small laceration. No signs of concussion." He frowned. "But she had me run an EKG, does she have heart problems?"

I shook my head. "Hypochondriasis. She's fine." I paused, a little chill passing over me. "Unless you found something."

"Nope. Heart rhythm is normal." He closed up his equipment and loaded it back into the ambulance. "But we'd like to take her to the hospital overnight, just for observation."

I nodded numbly and then climbed up to my mother. "Mom?"

144

I said softly. Her eyelids fluttered open. "You okay?"

She nodded. The white butterfly bandage stood out starkly on her face in the florescent light of the ambulance.

"You want to tell me what happened?" I had visions of her taking a tumble down the basement stairs.

"I saw lights in your apartment," she said, so much quieter than I'd ever heard her. I reached for her hand beneath the sheet.

"I left the lights on?"

"No. Not regular lights, bouncing little lights, like someone walking with a flashlight or a candle," she said. I froze. Someone had been in my apartment.

"About what time was this, Mrs. Harlow?" Bristol asked from behind me. I hadn't heard him approach. I looked back and saw him and Barnes standing at the foot of the ambulance.

"I...I don't know. What time is it now?"

"About nine-thirty, Irene," Mrs. Stokes said.

"It was after dinner, and getting dark outside. Maybe eight-thirty or so," my mother answered, looking around at us like we could tell her if that was the right answer.

"Can you tell us what happened next?" Bristol asked.

"I came over to make sure Rennie was okay." My heart squeezed at her words. If only I'd been home instead of hiding at the lake. "We've had a couple problems with the circuit breaker in the garage," she said. "I thought she might need some help, not that she ever asks for it." My cheeks flushed at her pronouncement, especially with the knowing exhale from Bristol behind me.

"But when I got to the top of the stairs, I knew something was wrong. The door was open, just a few inches, and then I realized Rennie's car wasn't in the driveway."

"You should have turned right around and called the Sheriff's Office," Mrs. Stokes interjected.

I raised my eyebrows at my mom.

She lifted a shoulder, ducking my eyes. "I didn't want to call them if it turned to be nothing."

"That sounds familiar," Bristol muttered.

"So then what?" I asked gently.

"I pushed open the door, called out hello," she frowned, "and then I don't, I can't really remember. Someone shoved into me, I think." She looked up at me, her brow still furrowed in concentration, skin puckering around the butterfly bandage. "Then I woke up in the entryway of the apartment with Joann telling me she'd called for help."

I sucked in a deep breath, trying to keep steady. She'd been so lucky she hadn't fallen backwards down those stairs and whoever had been in my apartment hadn't hurt her just for interrupting.

"Did you get a good look at who shoved you, Mrs. Harlow?" Bristol asked.

My mother shook her head.

"Maybe an idea of height?" Bristol continued in that deep, even voice that inspired trust. "Was he taller or shorter than you?"

"About the same, I guess, but bigger across. I think." She sighed. "I'm sorry I can't be much more help than that."

"No, this is good. It gives a place to start," Bristol said.

My mother looked to Mrs. Stokes. "Joann, did you see anything?"

"I was making Eddie lunch to take to work with him," Mrs. Stokes spoke up. She and my mother had been friends for years, though technically Joann, in her mid-forties, was closer to my age than my mother's. Joann and her husband, Eddie, who worked third shift at Smithery, had moved to their house across the alleyway almost twenty years ago. "I looked out the window and saw someone running down the steps from Rennie's apartment.

146

But no, I didn't get a good look at him." She rubbed her arms inside her robe. "So I told Eddie to call the sheriff and then I came out to have a look around."

"Doesn't anyone wait for us anymore?" I heard Barnes mutter.

"I saw Irene on the top of the steps up there. So I sat with her until you all got here."

"Thank you." My throat started to close up with emotion.

"Oh, honey. Me and Irene been friends for too long for you to do that." She reached out and patted my arm.

"Excuse me?" the EMT broke into our conversation. "I need to get Mrs. Harlow over to the hospital."

"All right." I wiped my eyes with my sleeve. "Let's go."

"Rennie, we need you to stay and answer a few questions." Sheffey now approached, looking a bit uncertain. "See what's missing from your apartment."

"My mother needs to go to the hospital." I glared at him.

"Rennie, you stay put. I'll ride over there with her." Mrs. Stokes patted my mother's shoulder. "Besides, Eddie leaves for work in an hour, and I don't want to be home by myself." She looked over her shoulder to my darkened apartment and shuddered.

"Mom?" I asked.

She scowled at me. "He said I'm going to be fine. Stop making such a fuss over me. Where'd you think you got that hard head of yours anyway?" For whatever reason, injury didn't seem to have such the hold on her that diseases did. So as long as the bump on her head hadn't resulted from an unexplained bout of dizziness that, in her mind, could be brain cancer, she seemed to have a pretty good grip on things.

"I'll get over there as soon as I can." I hopped down reluctantly, and the EMT closed the doors.

As soon as the ambulance pulled away, I turned to Sheffey,

Barnes, and Bristol. "All right, let's go."

My apartment had been tossed. I thought that was the word for it. Drawers were hanging open, clothing dangling sleeves or legs over the edge. Pots and pans, the few I had, were scattered all over the floor.

I reached down to pick up a picture of my dad and me off the floor—the glass in the frame had been shattered.

"Don't touch anything." Bristol's words stopped me just before I touched the picture. "We'll get someone out here from the crime lab with a print kit and see if we can get some fingerprints."

"Anything missing?" Sheffey asked.

"My computer," I said, after a long moment of looking around. "I keep it on the breakfast bar, and... Oh, God." My stomach dropped. "Fritzy."

Her cushion was empty. I ran to the bathroom to check the bathtub, where she hid when she was frightened by storms, though I had a heck of a time getting her in there for baths.

"What's wrong?" Barnes asked.

"My dog, Fritzy, Fritzsimmons. She's gone." I looked around the main room again, like I somehow could have missed her. I caught the glances exchanged between Bristol, Barnes and Sheffey.

"You think somebody took her?" My voice broke.

"Anybody threaten you?" Barnes made a face. "Recently, I mean."

I ran my hands through my hair. "No. Not unless you count my ex-husband, but he's not the type to do something like this. It's way too much work for him." I looked up at Bristol suddenly. "Someone's been calling and hanging up, and there was a note on my car a couple days ago, telling me to back off, but I thought..."

Bristol's mouth tightened. He knew exactly what I thought

148

about those phone calls and that note, and who I thought they probably came from. "I'll check it out," he said.

"Unless this has to do with Doc Hallacy," I offered hastily. "I've been asking questions." Maybe someone had gotten a little nervous.

I pictured Fritzy's big brown eyes, the scars on her sides from her days at the track and her hind legs bare from twenty-four hours a day in that little crate they'd kept her in. Tears filled my eyes. I'd adopted her to give her a better life, but now maybe it was worse.

"Rennie, I'm sure she's fine. She'll wander back here anytime now." Sheffey tried to sound comforting.

I shook my head, wiping my face on the back of my hand. "You don't get it." I moved past them both, grabbed a napkin out of the holder on the breakfast bar and used it open the cabinet beneath my sink. "Greyhounds are sight hounds."

"So?" Sheffey frowned.

"It means that if she can't see my apartment or a place she's familiar with, she's lost. She can't smell her way back, like most other dogs." I yanked her spare leash out, stuffed a handful of treats in my pocket, and grabbed her squawker. They'd used squawkers to call the dogs in at the track. I'd bought one in case Fritzy ever got away from me. I never thought I'd have to use it.

I headed for the door.

"Wait," Bristol called after me. "If someone's got a grudge against you for something, you're not safe out there."

My mouth tightened. "I'm going to look for her." I turned and headed out the door.

"Stay here, preserve the scene," I heard Bristol say to Barnes and Sheffey.

Bristol followed me down the stairs seconds later. I handed him the squawker. "She doesn't really know you, but she might come for this. If she comes toward you, yell for me and I'll leash her. Don't get too close or she might spook. She doesn't usually trust…strange men." My voice cracked, and I started to cry again.

"Rennie…"

I knew what he was going to say. That she might not be out here at all. She might be with whoever decided to break into my apartment and shove my mom. Or worse. "I have to look, Bristol, okay?"

He nodded. I started off down the alleyway.

"Wait." Bristol stopped by his car and popped the trunk. He handed me a high-powered flashlight.

"Thanks." I started calling Fritzy's name, a cold lump heavy in my stomach. Behind me, Bristol worked the squawker, which sounded like a monkey with its tail being pulled.

We split up when we reached Oak, the main road that our little cul-de-sac branched off of. He headed east and I went west, checking under trees and shadowy porches.

What if I never found her? What if she was hurt and died out here alone? My voice grew increasingly shrill as the minutes passed with no response.

I heard Bristol shout. I flew up the street to find him crouched over the ditch on the far side of the road.

"Oh, no," I whispered.

"I thought I heard something," Bristol said quietly.

I turned the light off so I didn't blind him and scrambled down. I heard Fritzy whimper.

"Oh, thank God." I knelt down beside her. When I touched her, she yelped and my hand came away damp.

"She's been hit, Rennie," Bristol said.

A sob broke free from me before I could stop it. "Help me," I begged him.

He touched my shoulder. "Stay here," he said.

Within minutes, he'd pulled around in the car. He opened the trunk again and pulled out an old blanket. He scrambled down the bank and spread the blanket out on the ground beside Fritzy.

"We're going to have to try to lift her into the blanket and then we can carry her like she's on a stretcher."

I wiped my eyes and nose, and nodded. As soon as I tried to touch her again, she cried so piteously, I yanked my hand back. "I can't," I whispered.

"Come on, she needs you to do this." Bristol grasped my hand and squeezed it.

I held his hand for a minute, drawing strength from it. "Okay." I took a deep breath and let go of his hand. Together we lifted her onto the blanket.

She cried something horrible, like we were beating her to death in the street, but we managed to get her in the car. I sat in the back with her.

Bristol flipped on the rollers and radioed to Sheryl at the station, asking her to wake up Dr. Robinson, the only vet in town.

Finally, ten minutes later, in the bright lights of the veterinarian's office, I could see all the damage that had been done. Her left ear had been nearly torn off. Her back leg on that same side was bent at an unnatural angle, the bone poking through her skin, bright white against her blood-soaked fur. Duct tape was stuck to her fur and wrapped around her collar.

"What happened?" Robinson helped us carry her into an exam room.

"A car, we think." I wiped my nose on the back of my hand.

Robinson took his time looking her over. He was close to my age, having taken over the practice from Dr. Seidel a few years ago. I liked him, not just because he was thorough, but because he, like me, was an outsider in Morrisville. I was divorced, and he was African-American. With certain folks in Morrisville, both of those were automatic strikes against us.

After a long moment, he looked up at me. "Rennie…"

My eyes flooded immediately. "I know it's bad. Just do your best, okay?" I smoothed the fur on Fritzy's head carefully, and she looked up at me with bloodshot and pained eyes. "She didn't deserve this." I leaned close to her. "I'm sorry, baby."

"Go home. I'll do what I can tonight," Robinson said. "She'll need surgery in the morning."

I shook my head. "I'll be at the hospital tonight with my mom."

Robinson frowned. "Bad night?"

"Someone broke into my apartment, knocked my mom down and let Fritzy loose," I said wearily.

"Oh, God. Will she be okay?" Robinson asked.

I nodded. "She's just in the hospital for observation."

"Get some rest. I'll call you in the morning as soon as I know anything."

"She's never been away from me before and…" I couldn't finish the rest of my sentence without crying.

"I'll give her something to help with the pain and take care of what I can tonight. She'll be fine, Rennie." Robinson gave me a reassuring smile, before shooing us out of the exam room.

"Hey, Doc, leave the duct tape for a few minutes, if you can. Don't touch it except with gloves. I'll send someone over for it later tonight, if that's okay?" Bristol asked.

Robinson nodded, an air of distraction around him. He was eager to get back to his patient, and I was grateful.

"You hoping to get a print off the tape?" I began to shiver as we stepped out of the vet office and headed back toward Bristol's car. It had finally stopped raining.

"Should be able to on that surface, unless they wore gloves." Bristol came around to my side of the car and opened the door for me.

Before getting in, I turned to face him. "Thank you for all your help tonight. I don't know if I'd have been able to do it by myself."

"You'd have made it." He smiled, shaking his head. "Every time I think I have you figured out, Rennie Harlow, you go and surprise me a little more."

"It's not intentional." I stepped closer to him, the door between us. Still, the mood immediately shifted. I could feel it heavy and crackling in the cool night air.

"I know," he said quietly. "But I like it."

"Too much," I supplied. I stepped just a little closer, my heart banging hard into my chest.

"Yeah, maybe," he said, his voice rough. Then he reached out and touched my cheek, his fingers moving over the tear tracks. I held my breath.

He leaned closer, his mouth a hairsbreadth from mine. I clutched the metal edge of the door to keep from reaching for him.

His radio blared, startling both of us. Bristol took a step back as Sheryl's voice rattled off a bunch of numbers.

"I have to go. I'll drop you off at the hospital." His voice instantly regained its professional edge.

"What's wrong?" I sat down in the car.

"Domestic disturbance over at the Radnor's." His mouth tightened. "Things have been quiet over there the last few months, but I knew eventually…" He sighed and closed the door for me.

I frowned. I'd had no idea it was that bad. Maybe that was one of the reasons Laura looked so harried all the time.

Bristol let me out at the emergency entrance to the hospital.

He pulled away before I could wave goodbye or try to figure out what else to say. *Although here wouldn't be the best place to continue the conversation we'd started in the vet's parking lot,* I thought, looking at all the hospital staff grouped around the ashtray stands outside. If anyone had seen us earlier, they couldn't have missed the signals of what would have happened, had Sheryl not called just then. I touched my cheek, where his fingers had brushed. The secret, not so much of one anymore, would have been out in the open and circulating about town in a matter of hours.

This town thrives on dirty little secrets like flies on dog poo. I shook my head as I walked into the hospital. In that instant, an idea, thin as smoke, suddenly flitted through my mind and evaporated before I could grasp it. Something about secrets. There was some connection there, but I couldn't quite get what it was.

Frustrated, I tried to put it from my mind—that was how things usually came to me—and walked to the registration desk to ask for my mother's room.

"Visiting hours are over," the woman behind the desk said.

"I know, but I'm her daughter. I just want to check on her."

The woman made a face as though she'd sucked on something sour, but she gave me the room number anyway.

My mother's room was dark and quiet. I slipped in, trying not to let too much light in from the hall. Once my eyes had adjusted, I saw Mrs. Stokes had stretched out in the bed next to my mother's. I made my way carefully to the armchair in the corner.

"Rennie," my mother whispered.

"Mom." I stepped closer to her bed. "I didn't mean to wake you. Are you all right? Do you need the nurse?"

She shook her head, a vague motion in the dark. "I'm fine." Her hand scrabbled across the sheets searching for mine. "I just…" She took a deep breath. "I want to say I'm sorry about this morning."

Guilt pulled hard on my heart. "No, Mom. It's my fault. You were right. It's none of my business where you—"

"I've started seeing a psychiatrist."

I sat down on the edge of her bed suddenly, my knees a bit weak. "What?"

"Dr. Murphy gave me his name a long time ago. I just didn't call him until a few weeks ago." She paused and looked up at me. "I'm just so tired of being sick all the time, Rennie. Of being worried all the time."

"Why didn't you tell me?"

She shrugged, a motion I felt from the movement of the bed rather than from seeing her. "I really wasn't sure if it would work. Even if it did…"

"You were too embarrassed," I guessed, judging by the sound of her voice.

"Things were different in my day. You didn't go talk to someone if you had problems…"

"Unless you were crazy," I filled in. "But things are different now, Mom. People practically wear their visits to a shrink as a badge of honor."

"Please use a different word. Shrink is a derogatory term."

My mother is back, ladies and gentleman. I smiled, although she couldn't see me. Probably better that she didn't, lest she think I was laughing at her. "All right, Mom."

"He's in Springfield, which is why it takes so long. But another of his colleagues may be opening up an office here in Morrisville, which would help."

"Is it making you feel any better?" I asked.

She sighed. "I don't know. A little, I suppose. I've only had a few visits. He says this sort of thing takes time. I have to learn that aches and pains are a part of life and getting older. That even healthy people have days where things hurt them." She paused. "I'm glad not to be hiding it from you anymore, Rennie."

"Me, too." I squeezed her hand. "You don't ever have to hide stuff from me, Mom, you know that."

"The same goes for you, though I doubt you believe me."

"Fair enough," I said lightly, trying to keep the conversation from veering into dangerous territory. I stood up. "Now, you should get some rest."

She pulled the covers tighter around herself while I settled myself in the armchair in the corner. Well, that was at least one thing off the list of everything bothering me, I thought, trying to find a comfortable place on the cool vinyl. I wondered when I could tell her I'd been faking her medicine the whole time. I thought of the uncertainty in her voice when she spoke of her psychiatrist. Maybe best to wait a few appointments more.

* * *

I must have dozed off, only to find myself suddenly awake, bolt upright in the chair, the hairs on the back of my neck standing at attention. My unconscious had done its work, connecting all the seemingly unrelated dots. What if Bristol and I had been going about this all wrong? Maybe it had nothing at all to do with someone gaining from Doc's death.

I slipped out of my mother's room into the hall and down to the lobby. I followed the signs to the hospital pharmacy, only to find a familiar metal gate closed over the counter and the door locked when I arrived at my destination.

I sighed heavily, linking my fingers through the metal mesh of the gate.

"Pharmacy's closed. Can I help you, hon?"

I turned to see a woman in scrubs with a cardigan thrown over her shoulders frowning at me.

"No, I was just hoping the pharmacist could answer some questions for me." I backed away from the gate under her watchful eye.

She squinted at me. "You one of Doc Hallacy's customers?"

I nodded, hoping she wouldn't recognize me further. Some of the nurses came from Litchfield or even farther to work in the hospital, maybe she was one.

"Too bad about him. Nice fellow." She nodded at the closed pharmacy. "Opens tomorrow at eight." She frowned slightly. "Better to stop by tomorrow afternoon if we'll need access to your records. We don't have them yet. Someone's going over bright and early to handle that." She leaned a little closer to me. "Can you believe it? All those patients, and his records are a mess from what I hear. The hospital is sending one of the young guys over, you know a real techy type, to see if he can sort out everything on that ancient computer. Sheriff's been asking for some information."

I tried to smile. My theory sort of depended on Doc's records and somebody being able to figure them out. "When did you say someone would be working on the records?"

"Tomorrow morning, I guess." Her eyes narrowed. "Hey, aren't you the one—"

"Thanks for your help." I walked away quickly before she could drag me into further conversation. I didn't want to talk about Doc Hallacy's murder tonight. The violence had hit a little too close to home.

Maybe, I thought, *I'd hit a little too close to home myself for somebody else's comfort.*

The thought left a prickling chill on my skin, banishing all ideas of rest from my mind.

FOURTEEN

"I can't do that." Billy, the junior pharmacist, as I'd dubbed him (he was actually a pharmacy technician, I think), looked horrified at my suggestion.

"I'm not saying you should give me the records. I'm just asking that you look around for me a little bit. It is a murder investigation." Not mine, but hey, it was early, even for a Tuesday morning, and I hadn't had coffee in over twenty-four hours. I couldn't quibble with the specifics, especially with someone who looked like Alfalfa from the Little Rascals and was probably only a couple of years older. Fortunately, he didn't seem to recognize me, which likely meant he lived outside of Morrisville proper.

"I already talked to the sheriff. He didn't mention any of this."

Not good. I held my breath and tried to look encouraging.

His mouth pursed into a frown, covering those slightly buck teeth. "What is it exactly you want me to look for?"

I fought the urge to throw my fist up in triumph. "Just anything out of the ordinary." I fiddled with the strap on my leather bag. "You know, like if Doc was giving people prescriptions that said one thing but were filled with another."

It'd occurred to me last night that maybe I wasn't the only one Doc did this 'favor' for. There could be others, maybe someone who'd found out they were being deceived and confronted Doc, as my mom might have one day. Or maybe he'd messed up and given someone what they'd actually asked for instead of the decoy. There were tons of possibilities, none that I could verify, if I didn't get Billy the Kid's cooperation.

"That would be illegal." His thin face flushed with color, highlighting the freckles on his cheeks. "Not to mention unethical."

"I know. That's why we need to find out," I said.

He narrowed his eyes. "What makes you think Doc Hallacy would do something like that?"

I played with the pen on the chain at the counter, avoiding looking at him. "Just a hunch." And personal experience.

"Well, if he did that, why wouldn't he alter the records to match?"

Billy had a good point, but it was one I'd already thought of. "No." I shook my head. "He'd have to have some way of keeping track of what was really going on, so he didn't make a mistake." Unless he had and that's what this was really all about. I hadn't read about any mysterious deaths, other than Doc's, so I was guessing not.

"All right," Billy said, reluctance clear in his voice. "I'll take a look."

"Thanks." I jotted my cell number on the back of an empty prescription bag. "Call me if you find anything." I'd decide then what to do. Telling Bristol at this point would have been jumping the gun, especially as I didn't have any proof to back up my theory. Yet. Once I did, I would have to explain I'd coerced Billy into giving up confidential information under the guise of an affiliation with the Sheriff's Office, something Bristol might not be too happy about.

Billy took my number and stuffed it in his pocket. I started to walk away and my cell phone rang. I dug around in my bag until I managed to fish it out. "Hello?" I hoped it wasn't Dr. Robinson with bad news about Fritzy or my mother with something wrong. After getting her checked out of her room at the hospital, I'd taken her and Mrs. Stokes home and left them both drinking tea at Mrs. Stokes' house.

"Rennie?" It was Barnes's voice on the other end.

"Yeah." I frowned. He sounded much too serious for Barnes. "What's wrong?"

"We need you to come down to the office as soon as you can."

My heart slammed hard in my chest. Something happened. "What's wrong? Did my mom—"

"No, no." He hesitated. "We've got a suspect in custody for the break-in at your place. Need to know if you want to press charges."

"Yes," I said instantly.

After an uncomfortable moment of silence, Barnes said, "I think you better come down here first."

I frowned. "Why?"

"Just come down, Rennie, okay?" He hung up without waiting for my reply.

I dropped the phone back into my bag and headed for my car. Despite Barnes's assurances, something was definitely wrong; I could hear it in his voice.

Why, I wondered, *hadn't Bristol called me with the news*?

* * *

"I'm not a criminal." Margene Bristol's face was red all the way out to her ears. "I demand you call my husband in here."

I stepped back from the one-way glass and stared at Barnes, who stood in the observation room with me. "You're kidding, right?"

He shifted a little, looking uncomfortable. "Her prints were on the door to your place."

"So? Maybe she stopped by sometime or something." Even as I heard the words come out of my mouth, I knew they weren't true.

160

Margene would have sooner eaten shredded glass than stopped by my apartment to chat. Unless, of course, she thought she might find Bristol there. I tried to figure out a way to say that to Barnes without revealing too much.

He hesitated and then continued. "There's more." I watched his normally jovial face twist. "Her fingerprints were found on the tape."

"The tape?" I asked, still not quite up to speed.

"The duct tape on your dog's collar. The fingerprints were hers. She did that."

Now, I knew why Barnes looked miserable. I turned back to stare at Margene, still sitting in the interview room with Sheryl trying to calm her down. "I can't believe it," I whispered.

"She hasn't confessed or anything. But Bristol thinks—"

"Bristol thinks she did it," I said flatly.

"Yeah."

"I'm telling you I didn't do it." Margene's plaintive wail pierced the relative quiet of the observation room. "I want Jake. Where's my husband?"

"He's excused himself from this investigation, Margene." Sheryl kept her tone even. "It's a conflict of interest."

"I'm not saying anything until he gets here." Margene started to slouch in her chair, then straightened her back, attempting a dignified pose.

"He's not your lawyer," Sheryl said, "and you don't have to say anything. We've got your fingerprints on the door and the tape on the dog's collar."

That got Margene's attention. Her facade fell away. "So what? Yeah, I was there," she said defiantly.

I heard Barnes sigh behind me.

"I didn't do anything illegal. The door was unlocked."

That was probably true. Dumb as it sounds, I wasn't always careful with the lock on my apartment. Partly because if someone really wanted it, they could just break the window and reach in, and partly because it felt so safe in Morrisville compared to where I'd lived before. Sometimes twenty-odd years of small-town living overcame good city common sense.

"It wasn't my fault the stupid dog followed me out. I just came over to talk to Rennie." Margene adjusted her v-neck shirt that v-ed a bit too low. "We had some…issues to discuss, but she wasn't home, so I left."

Sheryl tipped her head to the side, her mouth tightening. "The tape, Margene. We know the dog didn't just walk out on its own."

Margene's face transformed, color flooding in, her eyes narrowing to slits. "So? It's just a damn dog." She slapped her palms on the table for emphasis. "Maybe I wanted to show her what it was like to have someone take something away she cares about."

I stiffened, highly aware of the conclusions Barnes and Sheryl were probably drawing. Heat crawled up my neck and into my cheeks. Somehow my private feelings that had never been openly returned had just become a part of public record.

"I didn't hurt it any." Margene sniffed in disdain. "Just took it a few blocks over to the cemetery and taped it to a tree." She looked up at Sheryl, as if only just now aware of what she'd confessed. "But I meant to take the dog back. Only you came to get me this morning before I could."

"Doesn't matter." Sheryl's control had slipped a little. I could hear the fury bubbling up beneath the calm surface. I knew Sheryl sometimes still thought of me as the little girl she'd once been charged with caring for, and consequently, her emotion showed through more than it might with someone else. "The dog broke free. Got hit by a car last night."

Margene's eyes widened. She said, "No homicide for dogs, is there?" She tried to make it sound like a statement but it came out more as a question.

"No." I thought of Fritzy's pitiful yelps and bloodied body. "But there should be, you..." I bit back the last word, reminding myself that Barnes still stood in the room with me.

"What about the computer? You take Rennie's computer, just to see her struggle a bit with that too?"

"No, no." Margene shook her head vigorously, making her brown hair bounce against her face. "I didn't take anything."

"Other than the dog," Sheryl said.

Margene hesitated and then, looking a bit shamed, nodded.

Sheryl took a deep breath and looked at the one-way glass to us. "I think we're done in here."

Margene's head snapped around to the mirror. "Someone's in there listening? Who?"

Barnes stepped forward and snapped off the volume on the intercom that let us listen in. "We can keep her here for awhile. Trespassing, theft of property."

I winced hearing Fritzy referred to as property, but in the eyes of the law... "So you don't think she's the one who took my laptop and pushed my mom?"

Barnes shrugged. "We searched her house and her car, no sign of your computer. Based on your mother's description, we're looking for someone shorter and, uh, heavier."

I nodded, still not quite looking at him.

"We found another set of fingerprints at your place. Ones that match some we found at the pharmacy, but we couldn't get a hit in the system."

I frowned. "How come Margene's were in the system?"

"Bristol said she worked as a bank teller for a few months when they were first married."

The mention of Bristol's name and the word 'married' was enough to trigger another moment of awkward silence. "So you're telling me that there were two people in my place last night?" I asked to fill the gap.

"Sounds like." Barnes scratched his head under his hat. "You want to press charges against her or not?"

I looked back at Margene, still sitting at the table, but now eyeing the mirror suspiciously. Some of the color from her temper outburst remained in her face, and her shiny bob had become rumpled and mussed. As I watched, she seemed to sense someone looking at her, for she smoothed her hand over her shirt again, attempting to get herself back in order. For a second, I saw again that little trailer park girl, trying to fit in.

"No," I said finally. "I don't want to press charges." Fritzy hadn't deserved any of the pain, but maybe I did for coveting what didn't belong to me. There were rules against that too.

"Rennie," Barnes protested. I held up my hand to ward off further discussion and walked out of the room. "Let me know when you've got the other guy." He was the one I was really interested in, the one who might have killed Doc Hallacy.

I stepped out into the central area and almost paused when I saw Bristol, talking to Sheffey at his desk. I ducked my head and kept going, though not before I caught Barnes shaking his head at Bristol.

I hurried out the door, but not fast enough.

"Rennie." Bristol called out to me just as I reached my car.

I unlocked my car and got in. "I learned from this, Jake Bristol, even if you didn't," I muttered.

"You're not pressing charges," he said when he got within a

couple feet of me.

"Nope." I started to shut the door, intending to end the conversation right then and there. He caught the door and short of smashing his hand, I had no choice but to let the door hang open a little longer.

"Why not?" he demanded.

"None of your business." I glared up at him.

"She broke the law, Rennie. She deserves the punishment for that." His mouth thinned into a tight line. He meant what he said even though it was his wife we were talking about. That was just the kind of man Jake Bristol was, the kind of man he had to be in this job and love it as much as he did. I fought hard to squelch the pang in my heart for his pain, for my own. Even so, I felt sorry for Margene having to face him later today. Maybe that was punishment enough. I pictured Fritzy's face in my mind. No, it wasn't punishment enough, but I'd contributed, in my own way, to this end too.

"I said, no." I tugged on the door, trying to get him to let go.

He leaned down, a little too close for my own strength of will. I backed up from him slowly but not without the urge to move forward, and not before catching his scent, warm male. *Quit it, Rennie.*

"If it were anybody else besides her," his voice held warning, "you'd have—"

"Yeah, probably," I said, suddenly tired of fighting this, of fighting him. "But it's not, so I won't."

His brows drew together in a darkening expression. "Rennie—"

My patience dissolved. "Damnit, Bristol, I played my part in this too. She wasn't right to do that, but I'm not exactly guilt-free, get it?"

He pulled back, suddenly looking uncertain. I took the

opportunity to pull the door from his grasp and close it. Avoiding his gaze, I started the car, backed out of the spot, then pulled forward. Once I was on my way, though, I couldn't resist a look back in my rearview mirror. He still stood there, watching me in the distance, his hat shading his face so I couldn't see his expression. I knew right then I would carry that image of him with me always, and I'd never be able to remember it without feeling as I did in that moment. Like my heart was being torn straight out.

FIFTEEN

"Come on, Mom," I called in from her back door. "You ready? We're going to miss part of the service."

She appeared in the kitchen after a moment, tugging at her black cardigan. "I don't know, Rennie." Her hand fluttered up by her bandage. "I'm not really feeling too well. My head, you know, and my stomach...I'm getting these sharp pains."

I clamped my teeth down to keep from snapping at her. Headaches, though she had just cause for one today, and stomach aches were the most common complaints from those with hypochondriasis. Instead of asking me for some aspirin, she'd probably be scheduling a CAT scan for a brain tumor next week—that is unless her shrink, I mean her psychiatrist, could talk some sense into her.

"Mom, you're supposed to get out more often, right?" I tried not to let the irritation show in my voice. "Besides, I've got you covered." Reaching into my bag, I pulled out a bottle of Tylenol and a roll of Tums. I always carried them with me, though now for different reasons than I had with my career in the city. Sometimes I thought a career, for a woman, was only a euphemism for working twice as hard as any man only to get half as far.

"I don't know." My mother still stood in the kitchen, her hand pressed to her stomach.

"You want to say goodbye to Doc Hallacy, don't you? After all he's done for you?" The half of it she didn't even know.

She nodded, then scowled. "I'm not an infant, Rennie. Don't speak to me like that."

Despite her revelation to me about seeking mental help and our heart to heart immediately after, we seemed to be back where we always were. With me cajoling, pleading, begging, like a parent trying to talk a two-year old out of tantrum. Our roles had been reversed. I was now the mother attempting to convince her child that the monsters under the bed were rare and generally detectable in time to prevent death. I knew she was trying, but selfishly, that wasn't enough for me. I wanted her better now.

"Come on." I went into the house and pulled her out the door with me. "I've got a water bottle and a fold-up chair for you in the car."

"A chair?" She frowned. "No one except the immediate family usually sits at a graveside service. It'll look out of place."

I opened the passenger door and helped her in. "It'll be fine. Everyone knows you got knocked on the head last night. No one will even think twice about it."

Because they'll be too busy gossiping over Margene Bristol's arrest and the role another Harlow might have played in it, I thought with a grimace. I closed the car door for my mom and headed over to the driver's side. By now the details of Margene's crime would have been known to the entire town and most of the county. I was not looking forward to facing all those whispers, and especially Margene herself.

The drive to Oakpark Cemetery was less than a minute, even with traffic and parking. It was only a block from our house. That's where Margene, according to her own confession, had tried to tie Fritzy up with the tape. I winced, wondering if there'd be any sign left of Fritzy's certain terror at being out alone at night in a strange place.

I slung the chair in a bag over my shoulder, trying to keep it from snagging my hated pantyhose, and followed the fairly steady trickle of people into the center of the cemetery. Oakpark, as far as cemeteries go, was my favorite. A wide expanse of velvety green grass, dotted with hundred-year-old evergreens, and filled with intricate tombs and monuments. A life-sized angel over the grave of an infant, worn sandstone headstones in the classic tongue depressor shape with old-fashioned spelling still faintly visible, a miniature of a Greek temple, columns and all, presiding over the grave of several members of one family. At times it seemed more like a statuary than its more morbid calling. Maybe that's why it never bothered to me visit there as a child, even when other kids were too scared to even dare each other. As an adult, I found it peaceful more than disturbing. My dad's grave was toward the back, near his parents, with a space carved out for my mom, and me, if I wanted it.

I took a deep breath, inhaling the smell of freshly cut grass and heated pre-summer air.

"Stop that, Rennie." My mother frowned at me. "It's creepy."

Needless to say, my mother did not share my affection for the place. In her mind disease ran rampant in cemeteries, and like the kids who refused to breathe when passing by a cemetery, she didn't want to tempt fate.

I rolled my eyes. "All right."

The crowd had already gathered five or six deep around the coffin and the grave. We picked a spot toward the back. I extracted the chair from the bag and helped Mom sit in it, trying to hold it steady until she got settled.

As I suspected, no one so much as spared a second glance at her chair, but I got more than my share of questioning looks. In particular, Mrs. Mayor, Gloria Lottich, seemed to have lost track that the reason for the gathering remained in front of her instead of behind.

Finally, I gave her a big smile and waggled my fingers at her. She frowned one last time before swiveling back around, her sturdy black purse swinging in her hands from the abrupt movement.

Once Father Frederick got going on the eulogy, I took a second to look around. They say, whoever *they* are, that murderers often show up at the funeral of their victims. Unfortunately for me and my rather limited investigative skills, there appeared to be more than two hundred people standing around Doc's grave, in a loose semi-circle.

I began picking out faces I recognized. Even in a town of roughly three thousand, there were still people I didn't know. The odds of my knowing the person who killed Doc were pretty good, considering signs indicated Doc must have known him pretty well to let him behind the counter.

I found Arnie Ledbetter in the crowd, discreetly trying to take notes in a pocket-sized notebook. Max stood at his shoulder, whispering suggestions most likely. Principal Blederman, who'd hired me for the gym subbing job that had ended with me discovering Coach Swenson's body, was also there, along with Bruce Larrimore, the new high school math teacher (new meaning he hadn't been born here). Chief Librarian Estelle Harris, whose assistant had died in the attic in an auto-eroticism accident, stood next to Carl Rosen, whose bakery had provided me with birthday cakes every year until I was eighteen. Kitty Alexander appeared on the far side of the crowd, still looking rather put out over the whole parking space thing. Jenny Sturgeon, pale and unsteady, wearing a black dress that hung unevenly to her knees, stood near the casket. Even Marty Halpern was here, his wheelchair glinting brightly in the sunlight. Nurse Maude had apparently managed to drag him out of his house. Margene Bristol was noticeable only in her absence.

Swiveling a bit, I found Bristol and Sheffey observing the crowd from some distance back. With a chill skittering down my back, I realized there really was a good chance Doc Hallacy's murderer walked among us here. Bristol caught my eye, leaned over and said something to Sheffey, then headed my direction.

I turned back to face the casket, half-hoping he would get the hint. Still my heart throbbed a little harder with the sound of his approach.

"Can I talk to you?" he asked quietly, so as not to disturb the other mourners.

I shook my head, clenching the straps of my bag fiercely.

"Please."

My mother frowned up at him, deep lines carving into her face.

Those closest to us in the crowd started to turn and whisper amongst themselves. Ignoring him was attracting more attention than if I'd just gone in the first place.

"All right," I said. We walked back a few feet to stand near a large red-speckled marble headstone for the Sanderson family.

"Thanks for convincing Jenny Sturgeon to come in and give a statement," he said.

"I told you she knew something."

"Not the identity of Doc's killer," he pointed out.

I shrugged. He had me there.

"Anyway, I wanted to ask you something." He hesitated, then continued. "I need a favor."

I raised my eyebrows at him. If he was going to ask me to talk to Margene...

"I want you to talk to Laura Radnor."

My protest died on my lips at the sound of her name instead of the one I expected. "Why?"

"We picked up Jim Radnor last night for domestic abuse. He's done it before, about year ago, and a year before that. It's probably gone on even longer than that, but they finally got new neighbors a few years ago, ones who aren't afraid of the numbers 911." His mouth tightened.

"She moved out to her mother's place, but she didn't press charges against him. Never does. She'll eventually go back to him."

"And you want me to..." I prompted.

"Talk to her, try to get her to see we're here to protect her and her kids. She doesn't have to go through the rest of her life as a human punching bag," Bristol said.

"Why me?"

"Sheffey said you talked to her the other day, that she might listen to you." He shrugged.

I cursed Sheffey silently. "It wasn't so much a conversation as me asking her if she needed help and her blaming me for Doc's death."

"Still, that's more than she's ever said to any of us, even Sheryl." He hesitated. "If you'd help us out on this one, I would appreciate it."

Not nearly enough, I thought. "All right, I'll do what I can, but I'm not promising anything," I said.

He nodded at me. "Her mother lives at 642 Cypress. Thanks, Ren."

"Whatever," I mumbled.

Bristol walked back to the crowd, and heads turned to watch his progress. I grimaced and squared my shoulders, preparing to return to my mother and a whispered lecture.

I only got a few steps before the cell phone in my bag rang

shrilly. I froze. Father Frederick stopped mid-word and everyone turned, searching for the source of the intrusive sound. My mother looked back and glared at me.

I fumbled for the phone in my bag and got it out and open before the third ring.

"Hello?" I turned away from the crowd and headed deeper into the cemetery, my heels sinking into the soft ground.

"Uh, hi, this Bill…from the pharmacy." His voice lifted in question at the end like he wasn't quite sure who he was.

"Right. Bill." I made my way through the aisles, taking care not to step on graves. "You were searching Doc Hallacy's records."

"Yeah, and I found something." His voice lifted in excitement.

My heart tripped. "What have you got?" I tried not to sound too enthused. Didn't want to scare him off. People tended to spill more when you seemed less interested, something I'd discovered by accident while trying to conduct some of the most boring interviews.

"Labels," he said triumphantly.

"Labels." I paused, waiting for him to go on.

He took a deep breath, letting it out slowly, clearly seeking patience for my lack of brains. "The labels for prescription bottles?"

"Yeah, I understand that part, Billy, I'm not getting why it's important." I stopped walking about four rows from the funeral proceedings.

"It's Bill, not Billy. Doc saved the labels on his computer. Most likely so he wouldn't have to retype names and addresses over and over again. He'd just change the prescription information."

"But?" I prompted.

173

"Some of the labels don't match his records for the last medicine prescribed. Or they don't list a medicine at all, just the condition for which it's been prescribed." He paused. "All of this is highly illegal and unethical, you understand that."

"I'm not looking to bust Doc for a few bad labels." Actually, I wouldn't be busting anyone at all, but he didn't need to know that. At least not yet. "I just want to find out who killed him. What names were on the labels?"

He hesitated. "That information is confidential and—"

"Someone on that list may have killed Doc Hallacy," I pointed out.

He was quiet for a moment. "Okay. But you can't share this information with anyone."

"I won't," I promised, and I wouldn't. Even if I ended up with some good names, Bristol wouldn't take them seriously, not without more evidence than what I had.

"I found six. Karen Allison, the label says for acne, but her last prescription was for Valtrex."

"Which is used for?"

"Genital herpes."

"Oh." *Eew.* I could see why she might not want that medicine being recognized. Karen Allison was not a likely candidate for Doc Hallacy's murder, though. She was barely five feet tall and weighed maybe ninety pounds after a big lunch. She did work at the courthouse as a clerk, which meant no one would have thought twice about seeing her in the area that early in the morning. I added her name to my mental list of suspects. No way was I going to pull out a notebook and risk further ire from my mother.

"Margene Bristol."

My ears perked.

"Label says birth control. Last prescription in the system is for

Clomid."

"A fertility drug," I whispered. A pang shot through me. I turned to find Bristol in the crowd. The service had ended, and people were starting to file by the casket and pay their respects. Bristol stood with Barnes, surveying the crowd, eyes on the lookout for anything suspicious most likely. Too bad he didn't think to do the same thing at home. Though, it shouldn't have been necessary. It wouldn't have been necessary if... *Stop, Rennie.*

"Who else?" I watched people breaking up into groups in of twos and threes to go home. Max had stopped off to the side to talk to Bruce Larrimore, the math teacher. Whatever they were talking about seemed fairly intense. I recognized Max's body language, his fists clenched and his balding spot turning red, all the way over here.

"Next is James Radnor."

Laura's husband. He of the quick fists and little patience, or so it seemed. I'd never met the guy.

"Last 'scrip' is for Vicodin, but his label says Vicomins, get it?"

"Yeah," I said dryly.

"But here's the weird part. With the others, the prescriptions match up with the drug supply levels here, despite what the labels say. On this one, though, all the Vicodin is accounted for. So maybe Doc was really just giving vitamins and it's a typo."

Or maybe Doc had decided Jim Radnor had had enough and tried to cut him off. And in return, Jim Radnor had cut off Doc's life. Suddenly, my upcoming visit with Laura Radnor held a great deal more interest for me.

"Irene Harlow," Billy continued. "Her last prescription is for Xanax, an anti-anxiety drug. But," the frown was evident in his voice, "her label says for narcolepsy."

"Okay, next?" I asked swiftly before he made the connection between that label and me.

"Bruce Larrimore. Label says for headaches but it looks like…" I could hear him clicking on a keyboard. "…part of a cocktail."

"Excuse me?" I frowned.

"A drug cocktail, a mixture of medicines designed to work together to help the patient. In this particular case, one used to prevent HIV from turning into AIDS."

I jerked my eyes back toward where Max and Bruce Larrimore still stood arguing under the guise of polite conversation. My heart fell. "Oh, Max," I whispered.

"What was that?" Billy asked.

"Nothing. Never mind," I said quickly. "Thanks, Billy—Bill. You've been a great help. I have to go." I started to hang up.

"Wait, don't you need me to come down and give a statement or something?" He sounded confused.

"Not yet." I hung up quickly and turned my cell off. I didn't want Bill marching down to the station just yet. I needed to give Max, and Bruce, a chance to explain. Technically, anyone on that list might have had reason to be angry with Doc, especially if he'd threatened to blow someone's cover. Not everyone had been acting as strangely as Max the last few days, though. Maybe Bristol had been right all along.

I tucked the phone in my bag and walked back toward my mother, who was deep in conversation with Gloria Lottich. Neither of them saw me coming so I caught the tail end of their conversation.

"Gloria, she doesn't mean any harm. She's just coming out of a rough patch lately and—"

"Mom?" I said.

Both women jumped, startled even with my completely un-catlike approach. Heat soared up my neck and into my face. They'd clearly been discussing me and my indiscretions.

"I need to go to talk to Max for a minute. Are you all right here by yourself?" I tried to pretend I hadn't heard what she'd said moments earlier.

"For heaven's sake, Rennie, I'm not an invalid. I'll be fine." My mother avoided meeting my eyes, clearly aware she'd been caught.

I opened my mouth to say more, in defense of myself, but the decided against it. Speaking about it would only give them the sense they were allowed to discuss my private life amongst themselves. Closing my mouth, I turned and headed toward Max and Bruce.

Over Max's shoulder, Bruce saw me coming and said something. Immediately, the two of them split apart and started walking in opposite directions.

"Wait," I called out. "I need to talk to you. Both of you."

They froze, cringing like rabbits whose protective shrub has just been torn away in front of a pack of hungry dogs. Max turned and stalked toward me, his face a tight, angry mask.

"Listen, Rennie," he began.

"I know Bruce was there that morning," I said quietly. That was my guess at least. I didn't think either one of them killed Doc Hallacy, but I'd been wrong before. Better to confront in a public place, even if it was a cemetery, than all alone.

Max stiffened.

"I don't think he did anything wrong, but you need to tell Bristol what you know…" I paused and looked over at Bruce standing a few feet away. "What you both know. Because if I've figured it out, Bristol's not far behind. Then it will come out, all of it, in a big, ugly, public way, and you don't want that, either of you."

Bruce came a little closer, his steps skittish and sideways like I might take a swing at him. His tone was one of definitive outrage. "You don't know anything about what we want. I could lose my job over this."

I raised an eyebrow at him. "I've already lost mine.. In the meantime, a murderer still runs loose. So, let's just get this over with."

"Stay out of this, Rennie. You don't understand what's at stake here," Max said.

"No? Well, you better make sure Bristol understands it. Because if you don't tell him what you know, I will." I was hoping it wouldn't come down to that because I'd come by my information a little illicitly. If I had to, though, I would sing like the proverbial canary.

Bruce paled.

"Why, Rennie?" Max's fists were clenched at his side and shaking. "Why would you do this?"

"Because believe it or not, I'm trying to save your ass."

"We didn't ask for your help," Max said.

"I know. Consider it a gift, free of charge. From one former suspect to another."

* * *

"I'm telling you," Bruce said. "I didn't see anyone else there."

Bruce and Max sat together on one side of the table in the interview room, opposite Bristol. I kept quiet in my corner of the room, hoping no one would object to my presence in what was technically official business and kick me out.

"Why don't you just start from the beginning again, and tell me everything you remember. Don't worry about whether it's relevant or not. Sometimes people censor themselves and end up leaving out the proof we need." Bristol seemed deceptively relaxed, leaning forward just a bit in his chair, his hands steepled together and resting on the table. Only I, having been where Bruce and Max now sat, recognized the sharpness in his eyes, not completely hidden by the gentle tone of his voice or his deliberately passive body language.

Bruce looked to Max, his orangey-red pony tail sliding over his shoulder. Bruce was considered one of the most liberal teachers in Morrisville. Boy, if only everyone knew exactly how liberal.

Max gave him a reassuring nod, and Bruce straightened up a little, as if supported physically by Max's presence—another smart move by Bristol even though it wasn't procedure to have them both in here at the same time—and started talking again.

"I was running late, so I didn't get to the pharmacy until about seven forty."

About fifteen minutes before I arrived there, I thought.

"Doc usually left the back door open for me, the one that led out into the alley, so people wouldn't start wondering why I was going into the pharmacy so much or so early." Color flooded his pale skin. "I'm not ashamed of who I am or my condition, but people can be very judgmental at times when they find out, and I am happy here, finally." Tears brightened his eyes. "I love teaching and I didn't want to lose that."

Max squeezed his shoulder, and Bruce covered Max's hand with his, in what looked to be an automatic and familiar gesture, created by years together. "It's all right," Max said. "Keep going."

Bruce swallowed hard. "When I got to the pharmacy that morning, everything was still dark. The door was unlocked, though, so I went in." A tear slid down his cheek into his beard. "I called Doc's name a bunch of times, but he didn't answer. And then…and then I saw him laying there." Bruce pressed his fist to his mouth, shoulders shaking. After a moment, he drew a deep breath and looked at Bristol. "I know I should have called you, or someone, but I was just so scared."

"We're working on it now, Mr. Larrimore," Bristol said with patience. "What happened next?"

He shook his head. "I…I panicked. I ran to the front of the store to get Max at his office." He looked up at Bristol with pleading eyes. "You have to understand, I wasn't really thinking clearly. My first impulse was to get to Max. He'd know what to do. But as I opened the front door, I saw a car coming down the street."

"Rennie," Bristol said.

Bruce nodded. "I guess. So, I left, going back out the way I came. And by then I was really late. I had to get to school, I didn't want the first period kids waiting for me." He looked up again. "It just didn't seem real, what I saw that morning."

"He called me Friday evening as soon as he got home," Max spoke up. "I tried to get him to go to you and tell you what had happened, but…"

Bruce hunched his shoulders. "I couldn't risk it."

Well, that explained the argument I'd overheard and why Max was sleeping on the couch in his office, not to mention his sudden reversal of opinion on Arnie Ledbetter's journalistic skills. If he hadn't covered the story at all, that would have struck a number of people odd. Choosing incompetent Arnie to cover it meant he could protect Bruce without arousing too much suspicion, except from me, of course.

A faint frown crossed Bristol's face. "So what made you decide to come forward now?"

Max rolled his eyes, and Bruce looked over his shoulder at

me. "She found out somehow. She said she would tell you if we didn't, so…"

"Better that you get all the facts, rather than just the ones she knows about." Max shot me a grumpy look.

Bristol arched an eyebrow at me.

I shook my head. "Journalistic integrity. I can't reveal my sources."

He scowled. "There are reporters who have gone to jail for—"

"Are you threatening to lock me up for protecting my sources?" I demanded.

He sighed. "Rennie, I swear, you get yourself in over your head and—"

"What? You suspected Max. And I cleared him."

"Mostly." Bristol leveled a look at Bruce across the table. "You'll need to give us your fingerprints so we can eliminate yours from the scene. We'll also need to confirm your presence at the school with other witnesses."

Bruce nodded. "Principal Blederman saw me coming in."

"I do have one question, though," I said.

Bristol sighed again, and Max shook his head.

"Do you pick up your prescriptions every Friday, Bruce?"

"No, just when I need something. Why?" He frowned.

"How did Doc Hallacy know you were coming in that Friday morning then?"

"Oh." Bruce looked relieved at getting such an easy question. "I always call him the night before, so he can have it ready when I come by."

"So you called Doc then on Thursday night?" I asked. That could easily be verified by phone records.

He nodded. "Right when I got home from school, just before the pharmacy closed…" He frowned again. "Though he must have still had quite a few customers there."

"Why is that?" Bristol asked.

"Noise, in the background. Doc sounded distracted and there was someone talking loudly nearby."

"Did you hear anything they said?" I asked eagerly.

He shook his head.

I looked at Bristol and knew immediately what he was thinking. Doc could have had a confrontation with his murderer the night before he died, and because it would have been during normal store hours, the security cameras would have caught the soon-to-be murderer entering the pharmacy.

Bristol pushed back from the table. "Thank you for coming in, Mr. Larrimore, Max. We'll need to get written statements from both of you."

I started to follow Bristol out the door, but Max caught my arm as I walked by. "I'm sorry, Rennie," he said.

"You'd be sorrier still if I hadn't gotten you to come in here. They're far more likely to believe your story before you're arrested for murder than after." I stared at him balefully.

Max closed his eyes for a second. He was never very good with apologies, particularly to me. "Again, I'm sorry, Rennie. I was wrong to pull you from the story. I should have told you what was going on, but..." He opened his eyes and reached for Bruce's hand. "It wasn't my story to tell."

Seeing that tender gesture eased some of the hurt feelings in me. Max had tried to do a noble thing, protecting the one he loved. It just hadn't worked out very well. "I understand," I said.

"Listen, you can have full-time at the *Gazette*, if you want it." Max looked up at me, his dark eyes a little misty. "I'll figure out a way with the numbers. You've earned it."

I smiled at him and shook my head. "You know, Max, I think

I'm doing okay without it." If I worked for Max full-time, I was subject to his whims and his decisions, and I'd recently seen how well that could work. "So, no thank you. But I appreciate the offer."

He nodded, releasing my arm. "I'll see you in the office tomorrow?"

"Yeah, I can maybe stop by, see if you can dig up anything interesting for me to work on."

He laughed. I was serious. The Hallacy story might still have officially belonged to Arnie, but I was pretty sure I knew who killed Doc. Of all the names on Billy's list only one made sense with Doc's violent death. I called Father Dan and let him know I'd have to reschedule. I needed some proof to back up my theory— the videotape wouldn't be enough, even if it showed what I thought it would—and fortunately, I knew exactly where to go to get it.

SIXTEEN

"Laura ain't here." Gina Lorenzo, Laura's mother, squinted out at me from behind a screen door and a cloud of cigarette smoke.

The Lorenzo house was a small brick and siding ranch in an older neighborhood. The white paint on the siding was peeling off in large strips and weeds grew up in the sidewalk cracks. Toys lay scattered across the yard. Large smooth stones circled a brown and dead flowerbed in the front yard, but some were missing, like teeth out of a smile.

"Do you know where she is?" I asked.

Before she could answer, something crashed behind her in the house, and a child immediately began wailing. She hesitated, looking over her shoulder, and then kicked the door out to me, gesturing for me to follow.

I ducked inside, holding my breath as best I could in the toxic air in the house. Thirty years or more of cigarettes had polluted the entire atmosphere in there.

Gina Lorenzo scooped a little boy, one of Laura's, off the floor from amidst shards of a mixing bowl. She brushed him off while still clutching her cigarette with an inch of ash on the end between her two fingers.

"You here to try to talk her into leaving Jimmy?" She sat down and cuddled the child against her bony shoulder, blowing smoke out the far side of her mouth.

I nodded.

She shook her head. "A woman sticks by her husband through good and bad. That's the way it works. Her own fault if she made a choice she don't like now."

"But Mrs. Lorenzo…" I paused looking at the child on her lap and the other two staring zombie-like at the TV where a yellow sponge wearing pants danced around. "He h-i-t-s her." Probably nothing these children didn't already know, but better to spell it, just in case.

She coughed, a raspy, phelgmy sound that would have sent my mother running for a pulmonary specialist. "Jimmy's a decent man. He don't hit her but every once in awhile and never when she's pregnant." She paused to pull a piece of tobacco off her tongue. "Why you think she's got four kids in four years?" She cackled. "I taught her that. Had eight, myself. Every blessed one was a peaceful nine months before."

My stomach roiled at her words, and I stared at her, not knowing what to say.

"Four?" I managed to say. "I see only three." The same three I'd seen at the Sheriff's Office that day.

She nodded toward an infant carrier sitting on the floor near the kitchen table. I stepped closer and leaned down for a closer look. A beautiful, bald, pink newborn lay huddled under a blanket, like she was hiding from her new life.

In that instant, something pulled hard at my heart. I understood, just for a second, all those women who can't have children and take them from shopping carts, saving them from what they perceive as neglect or just disinterest. I allowed myself one tiny touch to the top of the infant's forehead, feeling that smooth skin and silky baby hair under my finger. A familiar stinging filled my eyes. I would never have children, but Laura Radnor produced them on a regular basis just for a refuge from her husband's fists. What a terrible life for her and them.

I stood and faced Mrs. Lorenzo. "Where is Laura?"

She avoided my eyes.

"The sheriff will come, Mrs. Lorenzo. He's the one who asked me to talk to her."

Her mouth pursed, creating a hundred tiny wrinkles around her lips. "She went back for some of her stuff. She's at her house out on Old Ice Factory Road."

I headed toward the door.

"But you'll never talk her into it. She always goes back to him. She knows her place."

The door slammed on Mrs. Lorenzo's final words. My hands fairly itched to go back in there and shake her until her brains rattled in her head. What kind of mother condemned her daughter to the same life she'd had? Encouraged it, even.

Some people should never be allowed to reproduce.

* * *

Laura Radnor's house was a green and white double-wide on a plot of straggly land. Someone, Laura most likely, had attempted to cheer the place up by planting flowers in an old tire beside the front door. Unfortunately, she seemed to have her mother's gardening skills. The flowers had dried to brown stalks already and the tire just blended in with the other debris lying around.

I knocked on the screen door. Behind it, the front door stood ajar.

"Hello?" I leaned forward to get a better look into the park model trailer. All I could see was a messy family room—toys spread everywhere, crutches leaning against the wall, a TV tray full of prescription bottles and next to it, a recliner tipped over on its side, a sign perhaps of last night's violence.

There was no response to my greeting. I pulled open the door and stepped up and in. "Laura?"

A flurry of activity caught the corner of my eye. I threw my hands up in defense and ducked, my heart nearly leaping into my mouth. A baseball bat whooshed through the air inches from my face.

"Stop," I shouted, keeping my head turned away. "I just want to talk."

"You scared me."

I looked up to find Laura Radnor frowning at me.

"I can see that," I said with a breathless laugh. She still held onto the bat, now angled off to one side.

"What are you doing here?" She twisted her hands tighter around the handle of the bat, the flesh making a squeaky sound as it slid over the wood.

Nervous, I thought. Probably should be with a husband like that.

"Sheriff Bristol asked me to stop by. Just to talk to you about what you're going through."

"Try to talk me into leaving, you mean." She lowered the end of the bat to the floor, wincing with the motion. Other than that, there was no other sign of harm to her.

She caught me looking. "He ain't dumb. He gets me where it don't show."

Without any encouragement from me, she raised her shirt. Fist-sized bruises, purple spreading from an almost circular point of impact, decorated her middle, which was still enlarged from her last baby.

"I-I'm sorry."

She glared at me. "You didn't do it."

Yet, she seemed angry with me.

"You could leave," I offered tentatively. "I'm sure Bristol would help you and—"

"Oh, it's so easy for you," she sneered. "Miss Fancy Pants,

187

college-education, leaving her husband. Shows how much you know."

Stung, I recoiled. Heat flooded my face and a thousand harsh words leapt to my tongue. I gritted my teeth and kept going. "I'm sure you're right. I don't understand your specific situation. But—"

"But nothing." Her hands reflexively clenched and released around the handle of the baseball bat. "I got four kids."

Which she wouldn't have, if she hadn't kept having them to escape her husband's violence. I thought pointing that out would not likely help my case.

"I don't have any place to go."

"Like, I said, I'm sure Bristol—"

She shook her head. "Jimmy gets good disability from the factory. What am I gonna do? Get a job? No one would hire me."

"You do what you have to, to survive."

She narrowed her eyes at me. "I'm surviving just fine. I didn't ask for help and I don't need it."

The desire to push out of there and let her wind up one of next year's tribute articles nearly overwhelmed me. Then I thought of that little pink baby, curled in her carrier, and of the older children made even older by what they must have seen. They deserved better.

"If you want to stay until he kills you, that's fine. But not your kids." I crossed my arms over my chest.

Her eyes went hard. "You can't take my children from me. They're mine."

"Not if you're putting them in danger." Disgust thickened my voice. "Then, they're not yours anymore or they shouldn't be." I lifted my chin, daring her to keep pushing.

"Nobody is taking my kids," she shouted, and with every word she advanced on me, forcing me farther into the family room. My foot slipped on a squeaky toy, throwing my balance off. My arms pin-wheeled, but I couldn't recover fast enough. I landed hard on the floor and found myself staring up at a red-faced Laura Radnor clutching a baseball bat like the last hitter up in a tie game. All of sudden, I was forced to wonder whether I'd pictured the right Radnor swinging that fatal blow to Doc Hallacy. Blood roared in my ears.

"You think you're so smart. Asking questions. Nosing around stuff that's none of your business. You've had it too easy." She started toward me, and I scooted back and knocked into the TV tray. Pill bottles rolled off the edge to land on the floor. The one closest to me, an empty, landed label up. "Vicomins." The final piece of the puzzle fell into place for me.

Doc Hallacy only made the fake labels for someone who might accidentally read them. I stared up at her. "You did it," I whispered. Her eyes went wide suddenly, and her grip on the bat slipped a little.

"I thought it was Jim. That he went nuts when Doc refused to give him more Vicodin. But it was you," I said.

She started to cry, which couldn't have surprised me more than if she'd taken a swing at my head. "You don't understand. It was an accident."

"You beat a man to death by *accident*?" I wanted to keep her talking, but I couldn't keep the disbelief out of my voice.

She shook her head. "No, no. It wasn't like that. Jim got the pills when he hurt his leg. He refused to take them on his own, so I broke one up and put it in his food one night. And it made him…better, more relaxed. Like what he used to be in the beginning."

"When he didn't hit you." I got my feet under me, but didn't stand, not just yet

"When the pills ran out," she said, swiping her hand over her face, "it was worse. So much more than it had been before."

"So you went to Doc Hallacy. Asked him to help you."

She nodded. "He did, for awhile."

"What happened?"

"He didn't understand," she said stubbornly. "I've got no place else to go. And…" She hesitated and then continued, "And no more babies. Dr. Murphy says it's too dangerous for me."

Probably not any more dangerous than not having more children, though Dr. Murphy may not have known that. "So you were just going to keep giving Jim the pills, but Doc Hallacy refused to give you anymore."

Tears spilled down her cheeks, tracks of liquid silver across the red plains of her face. "He told me, 'This is the last time, Laura. It's not right. He's addicted and needs help. So do you.'"

Doc found out she had every intention of keeping her husband hooked, it wasn't just a temporary thing to help her escape, and he had an attack of conscience. No such thing as black and white anymore, just a world of gray. He'd tried to help a young mother by giving her drugs illegally. When she'd stepped a little too close to the darker side of things, he'd tried to back away, but it was too late.

"I heard him on the phone, making plans to let someone in the back door the next morning." She looked up at me. "I only wanted another chance to try to convince him."

"So you went there early Friday morning?"

She nodded and wiped her face with the back of her hand. "I left the kids with my mom, and I drove over to the pharmacy and parked in the back, where the trucks deliver. The back door was unlocked, so I went in. I tried to talk to Doc, but he wouldn't listen.

He just got angry and kept telling me to go."

"So you hit him."

"I didn't mean to...but then I couldn't stop." She choked on a sob.

"What about the cane?"

"It's Jim's, for his busted knee. He needs a taller one, so I was returning it and..." She covered her face with her free hand, the bat still dangling from the other.

"You hung around for a bit...after, right?"

"Just to see if I could find the medicine. I didn't tear the place up none. That wouldn't have been right against Doc Hallacy."

Killing him was? I got to my feet slowly, never taking my eyes off of Laura. She seemed lost in her misery, the bat loose in her hand.

"I turned off the lights to keep people from coming in, but it didn't help. That guy with the ponytail came in, but he left right away. Then you showed up and started looking around, and I knew I couldn't stay to find the medicine. So I left."

"So you're the one who put the note on my car. And you broke into the *Gazette* and my apartment."

She looked up at me sharply. "I was trying to warn you. Get you to back off and leave it alone, but nothing worked with you. Not calling and hanging up, not taking your little computer, nothing." She hesitated. "I didn't mean to hurt your mama none, though. That was an accident."

"I can help you," I said gently. "Let's go in and talk to Bristol. You can tell him what happened."

Her expression suddenly grew distant, as though she could look right through me. "Oh, no," she said. "I can't tell anyone." She hoisted the bat to her shoulder again.

A chill slithered across my back.

"Neither can you." Her eyes were hard, like little glossy stones.

I began backing away. Problem was, Laura stood between me and the door. I held my hands out toward her in a placating gesture. "Now, Laura, think. Bristol's eventually going to come looking for me. He sent me out here remember?"

"Yeah, but I didn't know that, 'cause you never made it here." Her voice flat, she swiped through the air with the bat, and I leapt backwards, escaping her reach just in time. "There's an old well out back that'll keep you just fine."

"Laura, stop. You don't want to do this." Heart hammering in my chest, I feinted right, like I was going to turn and run down the hall toward the back of the trailer, then spun around and tried to dart past her toward the door.

The bat cracked down on my arm, just below my shoulder, sending a burning wave of pain over me. I screamed and stumbled to my knees.

She raised the bat again and I knew this time, this close, she wouldn't miss my head again.

I threw myself to the side of her. The impact of the floor against my arm made vomit rise into the back of my throat. The bat whistled through the air, missing me again.

I struggled to sit up. Agony electrified my body before I got more than a few inches off the floor. "Laura, stop, please," I whispered. Her determined face hung above me, upside down from my view. I didn't want that to be the last thing I saw in this world.

She took a deep breath and pulled her arms back, her elbows nearly behind her head. I flinched in expectation. Then I heard the most beautiful sounds in the world.

"Laura, put the bat down." Bristol's voice, followed by the sound of the screen door squeaking open.

Hot tears slid out of my eyes and down the sides of my face.

"Put it down, Laura," he said again. I heard him approaching and after a second, I could see him. He didn't look down at me, his attention focused entirely on Laura. "I don't want to shoot. You don't want me to shoot. So just put it—"

The bat slammed down toward my head, and I closed my eyes. The roar of Bristol's gun drowned out everything else. Warm droplets splattered on my face, just before wood smacked into my forehead with force enough to leave a mark, but nothing like what had been intended. I opened my eyes to see Laura Radnor, bleeding from a wound in her shoulder, swaying above me. She let her end of the bat go. It fell beside me with a muffled thump. Then she followed.

Bristol stepped forward, gun still trained on Laura. He kicked away the bat and handcuffed her before holstering his gun and kneeling beside me. "You all right?"

"My arm," I whispered.

He leaned forward, his familiar and comforting scent surrounding me. I had to fight against crying again.

He touched my arm gently, and I yelped. "It's broken," he said.

I nodded.

He let out a deep breath and sat back on his heels. He wiped his free hand over his face. "Christ, Rennie. You had me scared to death. I thought she was going to—"

"She was," I said.

He looked down at me, face solemn. "I couldn't...I don't know what I'd do if..." He reached out and touched my hair instead of finishing the sentence.

"Bristol," I whispered. Then I heard the sound of sirens approaching. He straightened up and his hand fell away from my hair.

"How did you know I was here?" My voice was cracked and uneven.

"I know you, Rennie." He gave me a tired smile. "Wherever you are, trouble follows."

"I mean it. How did you know? I didn't figure it out until a few minutes ago."

"Jim Radnor is over at the hospital, suffering withdrawal symptoms from Vicodin. He collapsed at Nick's, the bar over on Second Street. Problem is, he had no idea what was happening to him. We checked the pharmacy security camera tapes. It was Laura Radnor who was there Thursday night when Bruce Larrimore called, not Jim."

Outside, the sirens cut off and I heard doors slamming, voices approaching. "She tricked him. Slipped them into his food to keep him from hitting her."

Bristol nodded.

"What'll happen to her now?"

"Hospital, then jail, most likely."

Two pairs of EMTs knocked at the screen door and Bristol gave them the okay to come in.

"What about her kids?" I gritted my teeth as my set of EMTs shifted me onto a stretcher right alongside Laura Radnor's. "They can't stay with her husband. He may start abusing them."

Bristol shook his head. "Rennie, you are unbelievable. She tried to kill you and—"

"It's not their fault," I snapped. I couldn't imagine how frightened they would be when it was all said and done, something Laura Radnor should have thought of before she hauled off and hit Doc Hallacy...or me.

Bristol stepped forward, around the EMT trying to take my

blood pressure. "Every time I think I know you…" he said with more than a hint of wonder in his voice. He slid his hand, warm, calloused from hard work at his father's lumberyard, over mine, startling me. "I'll do my best." He met my eyes with surprising directness. His hand lingered on mine a few seconds too long, despite all those standing around to see.

That kept me close to bliss almost the whole way to the hospital. Well, that and the morphine.

SEVENTEEN

"Is she ready to go?" I asked Dr. Robinson almost a week later.

He frowned at me. "Are you?"

My arm, wrapped in a bulky cast from wrist to shoulder, rested in a sling across my good shoulder. I grimaced. "The best I'm going to get, at least for awhile, I guess."

"Well, Fritzy's ready to go home. Leash-walk only until I give you the go ahead. She'll need help on the stairs and in and out of cars," he warned me sternly.

I nodded.

He left the exam room, returning with Fritzy a few minutes later. Her fur had been shaved around the stitches on her ear and her side. She, like me, now wore a cast, though hers was on her back leg.

"Hi baby," I knelt before her. Her tail wagged and she hobbled forward, butting her head into my chest. "I'm so sorry." I stroked down her back, careful to avoid her sore spots and mine. Her fur, normally the odd, sticky-sweet smell of syrup, now held the medicinal scent of her surroundings.

"All right." Doctor Robinson handed me several bottles of pills and a sheaf of papers. "You've got her meds and you know what to do, so you're set. You'll need help getting her in your car, so give me a few minutes to get my next patient settled in and I'll come out with you."

I led Fritzy back out to the chaotic reception area, paid my bill, and then sat on one of the molded plastic chairs to wait.

The door sang its happy jingle as someone new entered the

office. I looked up to see Bristol headed toward me and felt my heartbeat sped up. We hadn't spoken one on one since the day in Laura Radnor's trailer, almost a week ago.

Laura had been taken to the hospital and now sat in jail, awaiting trial, as Bristol had predicted. Jim Radnor had been taken to Springfield to a clinic specializing in withdrawal. Their children were currently in foster care in separate homes. Their grandmother had a petition in for custody. 'Course, so did I.

I held Gina Lorenzo partially responsible for her daughter's actions, just by the way she raised her. I didn't want to see her do it again to another generation. It would be a few more weeks until anything would be decided. In a preemptive strike to the sure-to-come protest that my current living quarters were too small, I'd put in what I thought to be a low bid on the Parkmueller house. Jeff and I had worked out a deal. I told him if I got the house, I'd accept alimony equivalent to the sum of the monthly mortgage payment, which was a drastic cut from what he'd been sending. In exchange, he'd done everything he could, including sending one of his lawyer buddies down to expedite the whole process. I'd found out just yesterday that I got the Parkmueller house, junk included, of course. It would be a lot of work to clean it up, but I was actually looking forward to it.

Bristol wended his way through the maze of pets and pet owners to me.

"What are you doing here?" I asked.

"Your mother said you would be here." He tugged his hat off and held it in his hands.

In a surprise move, my mother had agreed to help me get my new house ready for human living again—I couldn't do it single-handedly. Literally. Now with a project in common, she and I were getting along a lot better these days, which was probably why she'd volunteered information about my whereabouts to Bristol, despite her disapproval of my feelings for him.

I nodded at him, still wondering why he was here.

He didn't say anything for a long moment. Then he took a deep breath and looked at me, the directness taking me by surprise. "I thought you might need some help."

I smiled, feeling a warm rush of pleasure. "Thanks."

He nodded, tapping his hat into his open hand a bit awkwardly.

He held the door for me and Fritzy and walked me to my car. I wanted to ask about Margene, to tell him what I knew about her supposed birth control pills. I hadn't revealed any part of the label ethics of Doc Hallacy in my story for the *Gazette*. If I told Bristol, I'd have to tell him how I got the information. Professionally, he'd have to be mad about my methods and personally, I wasn't sure that was a line he wanted me to cross. It was none of my business, really.

I unlocked the car and opened the back door. He lifted Fritzy onto the backseat for me. I'd stuffed blankets into the wells so if she fell off the seat, it wouldn't hurt her.

Bristol backed out of the car.

"You're covered in dog hair now." I gestured at his uniformed chest.

He made a couple of half-hearted swipes.

I stepped toward him. "No, you have to really brush..." I brushed my hand firmly down his chest a couple times, trying not to notice the heat of his skin and the firmness of his muscles through the shirt.

He caught my hand mid-motion. "I'm sorry about Fritzy."

I nodded. "Doctor Robinson says she's going to be all right. No limp or anything probably."

He hesitated. "Genie's really sorry, too."

Ah, so that's the way it was. My heart slowly drifted downward toward my stomach. I pulled my hand from his and my gaze to study my car keys, like I was trying to figure out the right one. "Tell her…" I closed my eyes, kicking myself mentally for what I was about to say. "Tell her it's fine."

I stepped back from him and got in the car. I slammed the door shut with him still standing there.

"Rennie." I could hear him through the closed window. Unhappiness bled through his face, pulling his mouth into a tight line.

I shook my head. He could choose to be miserable, but I wasn't going to go down with him. He'd made his choice, so I made mine.

I smiled at him through teary eyes. "Thanks for the help, Sheriff." I waved and then I pulled out of the parking space and back on to the road. When I looked in the rearview mirror, he still stood there, watching me go.

I felt better, lighter. There's nothing like death to help you get your priorities straight.

ABOUT THE AUTHOR

As a former award-winning corporate copywriter, Stacey Kade has written about everything from backhoe loaders to breast pumps. But she prefers to make things up instead. She lives in the Chicago suburbs with her husband, Greg, and their two retired racing greyhounds, Tall Walker (Walker) and SheWearsThePants (Pansy).